FRIENDS AND RELATIONS

Margaret Bacon

HEADLINE
REVIEW

First published in Great Britain in 1996 by
HEADLINE BOOK PUBLISHING

A HEADLINE REVIEW hardback

10 9 8 7 6 5 4 3 2 1

British Library Cataloguing in Publication Data

Bacon, Margaret
    Friends and relations
    1. English fiction – 20th century
    I. Title
    823.9′14 [F]

ISBN 0 7472 1710 6

Typeset by Palimpsest Book Production Limited,
Polmont, Stirlingshire
Printed and bound in Great Britain by
Mackays of Chatham PLC, Chatham, Kent

HEADLINE BOOK PUBLISHING
A division of Hodder Headline PLC
338 Euston Road
London NW1 3BH

FRIENDS AND RELATIONS

To Marjorie Paskin

Chapter One

'When we go up to Netherby next week,' he had said, 'we must celebrate. You choose yourself a treat.'

She had chosen something which wouldn't have been a treat at all to her younger self, in fact it would have seemed a ridiculous suggestion. But now it was a rare if simple luxury that she requested: a whole day to herself, to walk alone on the hills while he stayed at home and looked after the children.

As she set off at dawn on a misty May morning, the village was still asleep; not a sound could be heard as she walked down the narrow High Street between shuttered windows and closed doors. Even at the Newboulds' farm, at the far end of the village, there was no sign of life. When she was little, there always used to be a clattering of milk churns in the dairy and Mr Newbould would appear, stooping as he came through the low doorway, so that for a moment he seemed to be carrying the house on his back. Later she would see him going in his slow, unhurried way about the fields, unchangeable as the countryside around him.

The only time she had seen him looking out of place was on the day of his daughter Chrissie's wedding when he was driven in the village taxi, with Chrissie alongside him, down the High Street to the church. Chrissie had seemed magical in her white dress, mysterious behind her veil, but Mr Newbould had looked uncomfortable in his best suit and a shirt with a starched collar. He stared ahead with unseeing eyes, while Chrissie smiled and lifted her hand in a little wave like a princess, even to a pair of scruffy little five-year-olds, which was the age she and her friend Betty must have been, as they watched, wide-eyed and awestruck, as the wedding car drove slowly past the village green. They had never seen a bride before.

Old Mr Newbould was long dead now, of course, and his son had sold the land and gentrified the old farmhouse, converting the

1

dairy into an annex and replacing the old cobbles with concrete slabs, adorned with a wooden wheelbarrow full of bedding plants. Yet still, as she turned the corner into the lane which led up the dale, she seemed to hear the clattering of milk churns.

The lane had been modernised too, covered in tarmacadam for the first mile or so, before giving way to stones and grass. She could feel the difference under her feet, as she stood for a moment getting her breath back after the steep climb. Gone were the days when she used to run up here in order to get as quickly as possible to the stream which gushed down the Boar's Back, a long, flat-backed hill with a gentle slope at one end and a precipitous drop at the other, known locally as the Snout, a tumbling mass of loose boulders and scree.

Years ago, when she was about eight or nine, she and Betty had walked up here, swinging a picnic between them, ready to eat at the top of the hill, after they'd paddled in the stream and made their usual unsuccessful attempt to dam it. Betty had said, 'When I come up here with my brothers we don't go up the slope. We climb straight up the Snout. It's quicker.'

She was lying, of course; they both knew it, but what else could she reply except, 'So do I too, when I come on my own.' So when Betty had said, 'All right then, let's go up there now,' they were both committed.

It wasn't bad at first, plenty of grass and not too steep. Climbing swiftly to show she wasn't scared, she had soon been ahead. But suddenly it was steeper with not much grass to get a grip on, just loose stones on which she slipped and slithered, dislodging rocks with every step. Then it was so steep that she had to get down on all fours, her face almost touching the ground, hands and feet digging in as best they could. Her hands, as well as her feet, now sent stones crashing down behind her as she clawed at the scree, trying to get a grip on its shifting surface.

Suddenly she began to slip backwards and seemed to be taking half the mountainside with her. She managed to stop but could hear huge boulders scudding down behind her. There was silence, an eerie silence. She didn't dare look round. If one of the boulders hit and killed Betty, it would count as murder and she'd be hanged. It wouldn't be fair, of course, because it had all been Betty's idea in the first place. But they wouldn't know that, the judges and people wouldn't. And she wouldn't be able to tell them because it would be sneaking and she wouldn't be able to sneak even to save herself from being hanged, she realised in despair.

Then she heard Betty shouting, 'Look out, stupid, or you'll kill me,' and, weak with relief, she had lain on her stomach on the scree until she could see Betty alongside.

They had got to the top somehow, hands scraped and bleeding, no toes left in their sandals. They lay for a while, not speaking, on the short springy grass that topped the cliff. Then, 'Usually we go down by the path,' Betty had said.

Had they really done it? she wondered now, looking up at the precipitous scree. She remembered feeling very guilty, terrified that some long-sighted villager might have spotted them or that the vicar, anxiously surveying the church roof with his binoculars as he so often did, might have inadvertently got into his sights the figures of two children risking their lives on the Boar's Back. She knew that Betty was just as scared as she was, but they never said a word about it to each other. They must have been mad, she thought now. No, it's just that children have different compulsions. And we forget. Try as she would, she'd forgotten what it really felt like to be nine years old.

It shouldn't be like that, she thought as she set off again up the lane; we shouldn't forget what we once felt like, shouldn't let the truth of things slip away. We should keep it, preserve it, as a painter does.

The lane began to descend now and the scenery changed. Over the next ridge she could see the long stretch of marshland with Sawborough crouching in the distance to her left and Cumberside towering to her right. They had planned, she and Betty, to celebrate leaving school by climbing the two peaks in one day but at the last moment Betty had been prevented by verrucas. So she had gone with Luke instead.

They hardly knew each other really, she and Luke, a third year engineering student whom she'd met when she went up to college for an interview. They had nothing in common except a liking for long walks and the fact that he lived near Netherby, where she had been brought up and often returned for holidays. So they didn't have much to say to each other as they climbed, but it was so hot and the going so rough that it didn't matter.

She could still remember the strangely airless feel up here that day when there was no sound except for the clicking of the crickets

3

and the occasional desolate cry of the curlew. The sky had had a coppery look, very beautiful as they made their way slowly down the lane in the evening. The sun was no longer visible but its heat seemed to pervade the whole sky, scorching the earth beneath. It seemed to huddle over the land like some great bird hunched over its prey, she had thought as she trudged along, head down, struggling to find the right image for this beautiful, merciless heat which ravaged the parched earth with its talons. Oh yes, even then she had worried about finding the right words.

'We're in for a storm,' Luke, more practical, had said. 'We'd better move a bit faster.'

Even as he spoke the thunder began to rumble among the hills.

'We're going to be back later than we thought,' he went on. 'Will your parents be worried?'

'Not parents in the plural,' she told him. 'They're divorced.'

'I'm sorry,' he'd said, embarrassed.

'It's all right. Not your fault.'

'Well, will your mother be worried?'

'No. She went off years ago. I stayed with my father.'

'Oh, I'm sorry. I misunderstood,' poor Luke had apologised again.

'It's all right. I suppose it's an unusual way round. Not that it ever seemed odd to me.'

'Well, will *he* be worried about you?'

'Yes, he will,' she said, starting to walk much faster. 'Come on, let's get back.'

'Oh, no, I wasn't worried,' her father had said, in answer to her question. But she had seen the relief that lit up his face when he opened the door to her, the door of the cottage they had borrowed from friends in Netherby. She knew him too well to be deceived; he always tried not to fuss over her, feared to make her too dependent, too much the only child of a lone parent. He could hide his anxiety, but never his relief.

'There's no electricity,' he told them. 'It went off with the first crack of thunder. Do you suppose we could fry the joint on the primus stove?'

He was tall, donnish, rather helpless-looking. The helpless look predominated as he stood in the kitchen holding the roasting tin

4

with the pink leg of lamb in it. 'Not that we've ever used the primus stove,' he added.

'I'll get it going, sir,' Luke said. 'If there's meths and paraffin.'

'Oh, there'll be everything like that,' her father told him with a confidence that surprised her.

However, he was right and soon Luke had chopped the lamb into little bits and put the stove together, cleaned out the jets and lit the meths. The flames leapt up alarmingly but he kept calm and pumped until they burned low and yellow. The primus stove hissed gently and the kitchen was filled with its lovely, slightly acrid warmth, gradually enriched by the smell of onions and lamb stew.

'You're welcome to stay the night, Luke,' her father offered. 'The rain's pelting down.'

'I'd better get back,' Luke said. 'It'll blow itself out in a couple of hours. But I'll be glad to stay until it does,' he added, trimming the oil lamp and setting it down in the middle of the table.

They made her rest by the fire afterwards while they cleared the meal away. She'd imagined them in the kitchen, Luke organising things, her father with immense concentration wiping the dishes and then absent-mindedly dropping them back into the water. Neither she nor her father was in the least domesticated. He had always lived in his college, where she joined him in the holidays. They didn't cook their own meals.

Sleepily she'd listened to the men talking. Snatches of conversation drifted in from the kitchen amid the clattering of plates and cutlery.

'There is a point of view, Luke,' she'd heard her father say, 'which maintains that you shouldn't do unto others what you'd like done to you, because their tastes may be different.'

She'd smiled to herself, wondering what Luke was making of her father.

'Kate's a trusting kind of person,' her father was saying, as they came back to join her.

'Well, it's better than spending your life being suspicious of everybody,' she said.

'Is it?' Luke asked.

'Oh, yes,' her father told him. 'And I'll tell you another funny thing about my daughter. When she has a decision to make, she carefully weighs up all the arguments and decides what to do in a very rational manner. Then she acts on instinct and does the exact opposite.'

'I don't,' she objected indignantly. 'That's very unfair.'

'I'm not disapproving,' he said, smiling and reaching to take her hand. 'Reason is all right for unimportant decisions, but not much help when it comes to the ones that really matter. Instinct is a far safer guide then.'

'The heart hath its reasons which reason knoweth not,' she quoted.

Luke looked from one to the other; she could see that he found them puzzling, her and her father.

But he was right about the weather; when he left at midnight the sky was clear, the stars bright.

'We'd set you on your way, Luke,' her father said, 'but I'm too old and Kate's too weary.'

'That's all right, sir. Goodnight.'

'He's a nice chap,' her father said, when they went back indoors. 'But I wish he wouldn't call me sir.'

'It's only to show respect.'

'But it makes me feel so old.'

How old was he then, she wondered now, as she climbed up on to a stile and sat looking around her at the green and grey countryside, listening to the familiar sounds, the distant bleating of sheep, the crickets in the grass at her feet. He must have been forty-two. In twelve years' time she would catch him up. No, she would never catch him up: he would always be a generation ahead. Yet she would live to see things he never knew; even now, in 1978, she was taking for granted technology unknown to them both a decade ago.

She remembered how they had gone back indoors that night and she had talked, as she so often did, about how they would set up home together; once she was finished with all this wretched education, she had told him yet again, they would buy a house and live happily ever after. He had replied vaguely, as he always did. He was too resigned, she'd thought impatiently, too ready just to go on as he had always done. Well, she would just have to organise everything for the two of them. All the same she was hurt by his lack of enthusiasm and couldn't understand it.

But when suddenly, just after her Finals, he died of a massive heart attack, she understood. At last and too late, she understood.

He had known and he had never told her. That was what had made it unbearable. She could still feel the dreadful pain of it, the cruelty of not being told. Yet now, with children of her own, she understood and forgave. Wouldn't she herself instinctively protect Daniel and Paulette in the same way? But at twenty-one, she could only think that he should have told her, shared this dreadful secret, not let her go on making plans so blithely, so ignorantly, so heartlessly.

'He should have told me,' she kept repeating to Luke after the funeral, when he was alone with her in her father's rooms. 'I don't even know what he wants me to do with his things . . .'

She couldn't go on. She was sobbing in Luke's arms.

'I'll help you,' he said. 'We'll do it together. You're exhausted now.'

He calmed her, made her lie down, brought her tea.

He sat on the side of the bed.

'Kate,' he said. 'Let me look after you. Please. You know I've always wanted to marry you.'

Did she know? she wondered. A vague idea that he had mentioned something about it one day as they walked on the hills came into her mind, but she hadn't taken much notice at the time, it hadn't been part of her scheme of things.

'I haven't much money yet,' Luke was saying, 'but we could manage somehow, make a home together. It's not much to offer, but—'

'Sh, Luke, it's nothing to do with that.'

'Just let me look after you, that's all I want. Please.'

'No, you don't marry people so that they can look after you.'

All the same she was tempted. He was a good friend. He had known her father. She was fond of him. She would belong in the world again if she was with Luke. Without him she was now a stray thing, unrelated to anyone.

'Your mother didn't send a message?' he asked, reading her thoughts.

'No, I wouldn't have wanted her to. Anyway she didn't. She's been told. Solicitors, you know.'

'You've no other relations?'

She shook her head.

'Please, Kate.'

'I've got to manage on my own, Luke.'

'Why?'

How could she explain? Of course it was tempting, the thought of having his comfort and companionship, his love, his under-standing, his shared memories of her father. But her reason told her that it would be cowardly to give in to that temptation. Take, take, take, that's all it would be. And it would just be because she wasn't strong and independent enough to bear it all, face it all, on her own. Besides, they hardly knew each other and they'd nothing in common; he was a scientist, she very much an arts kind of person.

Yet still, she ached to say yes. Not to hurt him. Above all, not to inflict pain, the awful pain of rejection. When people die they reject you. She had run her hand through her father's hair as he lay in the morgue and he hadn't even smiled.

It struck her now, for the first time, as she sat on the stile, that her father had been right. He'd said that she always reasoned things out before making a decision and then acted on impulse and did the opposite of what reason told her. She had done exactly that: she had worked out all the reasons for not marrying Luke, then gone ahead and married him.

She had done it almost immediately, too, because the next month he had been asked to go and work abroad for two years in Sri Lanka. He'd gone off the day after their quiet registry office wedding and she had followed two weeks later.

Looking back on them now, those two years seemed a thing apart from the rest of her life, existing in a little world of their own, a world in which everything was strange, new and surprising. The very heat of the place, when she arrived, came as a shock to one whose idea of warmth was a hot summer's day on Cumberside. And the landscape, too, had seemed strange and exotic. As she sat now among these gentle hills, patterned with dry-stone walls and dotted with sheep and boulders, she saw again in her mind's eye those watery fields of paddy, which she had first glimpsed from a train window on that slow, day-long journey across the country, and the women working in them, ankle deep in water, as they stooped to do their planting, their skirts tucked up between their knees and their heads bound in bandannas. They glanced up as the train passed and, looking back into those glimpsed faces, she had felt like an intruder in their world.

She had grown to love that strange new world with its misty mornings and warm, velvety evenings, heavy with the scent of tropical flowers. She had grown familiar with it in the next two years, as she explored the ruins of its old cities, found great statues of the Buddha hidden in the depths of woods in remote places, seen strange creatures and exotic birds. She grew accustomed to it all, so that it no longer seemed strange to see wide-horned buffalo doing the work of horses, or elephants toiling on building sites.

She had observed herself also in those two years, changing, coming to terms with her father's death, beginning to dare to remember him, at first tentatively, fearful of pain, then gradually with joy. She grew to love and trust the husband whom she had so precipitately married; she saw him grow in confidence, saw that he was respected by his colleagues, liked by his boss. And by a strange coincidence, when she was introduced to that same boss's wife, found herself shaking hands with Chrissie Newbould, last seen when she herself was a little girl in Netherby and Chrissie a bride on her way to church.

They had worked together, she and Chrissie, in the village hospital and when, by accident, she had conceived, she asked Chrissie to be the baby's godmother. Daniel was born in a little maternity home run by nuns, where a local woman came to squat in the corner of the room and wail, presumably in order to drown any of the noises which might come from the labouring mother. So there were three of them to travel back to England at the end of their two years. Three-and-a-half really, because she was pregnant again, with Paulette.

In a way, she reflected as she sat on the stile in the hills above Netherby now, it had been almost as strange coming back to England as going abroad had been. Luke's firm had sent them to Yorkshire to work on a water purification scheme. Of course it had been lovely to be back in the north, able to get to Netherby, walk again on the hills of her childhood, now with children of her own. But all the time the memory of those two years abroad lived on in her and she had seemed for a while to see her own country through a stranger's eyes. 'What was it like in Sri Lanka?' people kept asking and as she repeated herself she realised guiltily that it was becoming blurred, as if memory was making it all nostalgic, false even.

It had come to her that she must write it all down as precisely as she could, try to recapture it exactly as it was, with the surprise of it, the shock of the heat, the cool beauty of the evening, the serenity of the Buddhas and the sybaritic pleasure with which the elephants sank into the water when they were taken to the river, rolling their great bodies in voluptuous abandon, little eyes closed in ecstasy, ears flopping on the water like collapsed tents.

She realised that she must relive it all, so that she could see and hear and feel it all again, with the surprise still in it, otherwise she would not be telling it as it really was.

It was not a very convenient time, not now that she had a baby girl as well as the two-year-old Daniel. The writing would just have to be done at night. So she didn't mind when Luke said he would have to be away on site all the week, for at least six months only home at weekends. She saw on his face that he was expecting her to be upset and, though relieved by her reaction, or lack of it, was also a little hurt. She would have liked to explain, but dared not; it was all too secret, and besides she didn't know if she could do it, just that she had to try.

She had started writing at seven o'clock that first night and she worked until two o'clock the next morning. She'd thought that looking after little children all day was tiring but soon realised that everything about her was tired, except her mind: the children might be emotionally and physically demanding, but had made little demand on the brain. Her brain had been having a restful time just now; it wouldn't be expecting too much of it to spend six hours enabling her to recall, relive, analyse, describe – and write.

But the most difficult part was the reliving. She needed to escape into a kind of reverie or rather a different reality. But sometimes there seemed to be a door which she couldn't unlock. She would find herself in the wrong garden. When she wanted to feel again the magic of the tropical sky at night, here where the stars were outshone by suburban street lights, she shut her eyes and willed herself elsewhere, under a tropical moon. But she found herself under other skies, or rather a particular night sky of her childhood.

Years ago, when they were about ten, Betty and she had begged to be allowed, one very hot summer, to sleep outside under the stars. Betty's house had a huge and rambling garden. It was to be theirs for the night, nobody was to intrude, grown-ups were banned.

It took them a long time to decide where to put their camp beds. They dragged them into the orchard, but decided it was too shady so tried the vegetable garden instead, but the compost heap smelled horrible. In the end they brought them back to where they had started in the middle of the lawn.

'We'll get as much air as possible here,' Betty had said. 'And if we're attacked we'll be able to see who it is.'

There were some plant pots by the toolshed; Betty said she'd read that if you turned a plant pot upside down over a candle you could cook on it.

'We could make hot cocoa like that,' she said. 'If we had any cocoa. I think they've gone out,' she added.

They crept up to the house and found an old pan in a kitchen drawer, milk in the larder and a half-empty tin of damp and lumpy cocoa in a cupboard. Candles and matches were no problem: the electricity was always failing and there were candles lying about all over the place.

'It's bound to be fairly slow,' Betty pointed out, as they balanced the pan over the little hole in the plant pot. 'We might as well put it on now.' They left it wobbling there in the toolshed while they put the two little camp beds on the lawn.

'I'm not spying or anything,' Betty's mother said, coming down the path. 'I just thought you might like hot water bottles. It might feel cold later on.'

They could hardly bring themselves to reply. After she had gone, Betty held the offending bottles at arm's length and apologised for her mother. 'She means well,' she explained, 'it's just that she doesn't understand anything.'

The sky was huge; it seemed to fill the whole world. The garden shrank to nothing beneath it. How could you describe it, she had wondered, gazing up into the vastness of it? All the light was up there, down here were only shadows. The stars, each and every one, shone with a clear and brilliant light and there were millions of them. Millions and millions, as far as she could see, above, around and beyond, because they went deeper and deeper into the darkness, which was not at all a solid thing, but a kind of blue space that went on for ever.

She lay gazing at it all, hearing Betty's gentle breathing until she herself drifted into sleep.

They both woke in the early hours of the next morning feeling very cold.

'I expect the milk's boiling by now,' Betty said, and they went, shivering in their thin nighties, the grass cold and wet with dew under their bare feet, back into the shed. The milk was still tepid, apparently unaffected by the candle which flickered beneath it under the plant pot.

'We could use the water in one of those,' Betty said, pointing at the despised hot water bottles.

She could remember it still, the rubbery taste of the lumpy, tepid cocoa which they'd made with the water from those bottles long ago.

It hadn't been a good evening's writing, she remembered thinking, as she struggled to write her first book: she had hoped to relive the magic of a tropical night but all her memory had come up with was rubbery cocoa. It seemed as if once she opened herself up to the past, other memories crowded randomly in. Sometimes she had felt as if she was entering some long unvisited attic and finding it full of forgotten treasures but couldn't find what she came to seek. But perhaps, she had consoled herself that night, those two skies had something in common; the vastness and the depth and her own sense of wonder.

She had worked every night until two or three o'clock in the morning when either she fell asleep at her desk or the baby cried and she had to stop thinking of words but of milk and clean nappies. Then she fell into bed, utterly weary but somehow relaxed. And so it went on, month after month until the book was finished.

It had taken her a year to write it, but it took another four years to get it published, by which time she'd written her first novel, the children were both at school and Luke had told her that the firm wanted him to move down south.

'It's to set up a regional office in Wiltshire, so we'll be settled for a while.'

'And nearer Chrissie too,' she'd said, peering at Daniel's school atlas.

The children were less than delighted when the travel book came out. Six-year-old Paulette came home from school distraught. 'She pinned it up on the board, that thing about you in the paper. On the board where we have our news, Miss Carlton did.'

She choked and added, 'And now everyone will know.'

Daniel didn't give way to tears, but looked at her resentfully and said, 'It's not very nice for a chap when all his mates read about his mother.'

Only Luke seemed pleased. He was delighted for her, couldn't understand why she'd been so reticent about it, almost afraid of telling him. She'd thought he would want her to get a proper paid job but had known that, if she did, the writing would get squeezed out.

His support was instant.

'But writing *is* a proper job,' he told her. 'Of course you must give it all the time you've got. And when we go up to Netherby next week, we must celebrate. You choose yourself a treat.'

So she had chosen to be allowed a day by herself walking on the hills while he amused the children back in the cottage which they always rented.

'Done,' he had said. 'And I'll get them off to bed early and have a gala supper ready for you when you get home.'

It was time to get back for that special supper, she thought now, taking a last look round at the hills before climbing off the stile and descending into the lane. She looked across at the Boar's Back. Had they really climbed that cliff face? The very thought that Daniel and Paulette might ever do such a thing made her shiver. And the way she'd married a man she scarcely knew, that made her shiver too at the foolhardiness of her younger self.

The light was fading by the time she reached the village and the air was beginning to feel damp. Luke had lit a fire, and a smell of lamb cooking with rosemary filled the cottage.

'You go and have a bath,' he told her as he kissed her, and added, 'I've exhausted the kids, stuffed them full of shepherd's pie and now they're both sound asleep in bed.'

'And I've had a wonderful time,' she said, leaning against him and resting her head on his shoulder. 'It was so peaceful up there. And, do you know, I haven't seen a soul all day.'

There was a bottle of wine on the table, when she came down, and lighted candles.

The candles reminded her of something. She told him about

13

Betty and trying to boil milk over a candle under an upturned plant pot.

'You didn't really believe it would work, did you?'

'Oh, yes. Betty had read about it. We believed everything we saw in print.'

'You don't keep in touch, do you?'

She shook her head.

'Just cards at Christmas. I expect she remembers that night under the stars though. They've given me six copies of the book. Maybe I'll send her one.'

Chapter Two

There weren't many things about Betty which annoyed Colin, but this was one of them: this habit of hers of not opening letters and parcels until she'd worked out who sent them. She wasted precious minutes studying handwriting, squinnying at indecipherable postmarks, looking for clues, instead of just opening up and finding out.

She was doing it now, turning the parcel round in her hands, puzzling over the printed address.

'Oh, just open the damned thing,' he advised.

'It could be Kate,' she remarked, as if he hadn't spoken.

'Who's Kate?'

'Her printing was like that at school; I remember it on exercise books.'

Neatly and methodically she opened the parcel, her long capable fingers swiftly disposing of staples and sellotape. She did everything quickly, he had often observed, then frittered away the time saved by such things as trying to guess who'd sent letters. She read *The Times* very fast and then wasted half an hour doing the crossword, another time-consuming occupation of which he disapproved.

She had taken the book out of the paddibag at last.

'Well done, Kate,' she said. 'She's written a travel book. They've given her a good cover,' she added, holding the book at arm's length and nodding approvingly. Then she settled down to read just as if he wasn't there. But, 'We were friends when we were little and at school together for a while in Netherby,' she remarked suddenly, answering his question at last. 'We send cards at Christmas, but haven't really kept in touch. Last time I saw her was at her father's funeral years ago and I'm not sure she took on board who I was then. She was terribly stricken, poor thing.'

She was lost in the book already, reading swiftly as she always did, so much so that he had sometimes in the past found it hard to believe that she really had read something and had tested her by asking tricky questions. But she always knew the answers. Oh, she was clever all right. She had read English at Oxford but decided that there was no money in it and taken up accountancy instead. Then she'd changed to law. She was that rare thing, he thought, a woman both literate and numerate.

The life he planned for himself required a clever wife. The others, in what they jokingly called the Mafia, had each acquired one. They were all well on the way already. He himself had used his university years to advantage, made his mark in the Union, been active in politics, made many useful contacts. The legal practice was going well, he should be a partner next year. Or he might go into the City. Overtures had been made. He looked around the flat with satisfaction; not bad to be in a luxury flat in Kensington at his age and considering his beginnings, which nowadays actually he preferred not to do. And there was a real chance of being a parliamentary candidate next time round.

The timing would be right. Timing was everything in politics. You must catch the tide. He still sweated when he thought of the speech he'd made for the Young Conservatives at that party conference in the early Seventies. He remembered holding forth in favour of inflation, echoing the Chancellor. Inflation was an obsession of the socialists, he'd declaimed, they were always on about keeping prices down, worrying about the consumer. His was the party of the producer and there would be no profits for the producer unless prices were let rip. Off with controls, he'd said, shift income tax to this new VAT, and they'd all cheered. Cheered him to the roof, called him promising, a rising young star.

Then it all went wrong. Incredibly in just four years they'd managed to treble inflation, sending it soaring into double figures. He remembered the panic among the great and powerful figures he had worshipped. He remembered the three-day week. They'd made a fearful mistake. He hadn't gone to that final conference; he'd kept very quiet about his politics. Certainly he hadn't wanted to find a seat then. Let somebody else clear up the mess.

Now the time was ripe. The electorate had had time to forget. He wouldn't be held responsible. History was being rewritten anyway. Nobody remembered being the party of inflation. Certainly no conference-goer remembered what they had once cheered; they would happily cheer the opposite now. Good times lay ahead for an ambitious man. Which brought him back to thinking of Betty.

She'd look great sitting next to him on any platform. She was beautiful, with that fine skin that goes with fair hair and green eyes if you're lucky. She was lucky. And the body too, that was something spectacular. And he was lucky, to share it. And her enthusiasm in bed was quite something to share, he reflected, watching her now, imagining the body under the negligee. She was laughing and he watched appreciatively as the flesh moved, gently shaking beneath the flimsy material.

Yes, Colin thought, she was beautiful and clever, sophisticated and tolerant and had a great sense of humour. She responded to a challenge too and that was always a plus in a politician's wife. And there was a quality of endurance about her, which might also be necessary. All in all, maybe he should marry her.

Betty lay in the bath, a glass of wine alongside, and finished Kate's book. Her idea of heaven was not the eating of pâté de foie gras to the sound of trumpets, but lying in a hot bath with a drink and a good book. And Kate's book was good. She'd obviously cared about the place, had been moved by it and she conveyed it well, the beauty and the excitement of it all, with a sense of surprise which made everything seem fresh and intriguing. She didn't patronise. Unlike most travel writers, she hadn't gone deliberately to the place to use it for her writing, she'd just felt moved to capture the experience after she got back.

Betty manoeuvred her toe round the tap to add more hot water, took another sip of wine and lay back and thought about Kate.

She had always envied her really when they were children. For a start Kate's situation was more interesting than her own. There was something mysterious about Kate's parents. She didn't know what it was exactly, but had observed that if her mother and her friends happened to be talking about Kate, they stopped when Betty came in. Reference to Kate's mother brought on disapproving looks and that funny tense feeling in the atmosphere that put you on your guard but you didn't know why. Her parents always seemed to give Kate an extra special welcome and treated her more gently than they did their own children. They treated Kate like a visitor, which she wasn't because she'd come round to play for as long as anyone could remember and so was really part of the household.

Kate was an only child and that too made her more interesting. Apart from being saddled with ordinary parents she, Betty, had three older brothers. She used to think that she was probably an afterthought, a mistake. They teased her. Even when she had her plaits cut off they still pulled her hair. She envied Kate her lack of brothers.

Kate was pretty, of course, and though grown-ups say that looks don't matter, they do in fact prefer pretty children. She herself was a very plain child with her dead straight hair, her pale face and green eyes under non-existent eyebrows. She had one of those pointed little faces that make you look sly. Kate's face was of the flatter variety, with wide-spaced eyes, huge and violet-blue. There was a childish chubbiness not just about Kate's face but her body too, which appealed to the grown-ups who were inclined to cuddle her. She herself was very thin and tall for her age with long, long legs. She was spiky, she knew it, and about as cuddly as a stick insect.

Of course, they'd soon learned to cash in on Kate's looks; if they wanted any favours from the adult world they always sent Kate to solicit them. Oh yes, they were crafty enough, though Kate wasn't nearly as crafty as she was. At Christmas they didn't give each other presents; instead they had an arrangement whereby they could go to each other's bookcase and choose whatever book they wanted. She always hid her favourites before she let Kate into her bedroom to choose. Kate never realised.

She smiled as she remembered; she hadn't thought about those days for so long and had quite forgotten about the books at Christmas.

But she did remember how she used to look at her own unprepossessing self in the mirror and defiantly pull faces at her ugly reflection to make herself look even worse. She didn't care. She'd got Bisto.

Bisto was her dog and she told him everything.

She had always wanted a dog. Her parents had held out for years on the flimsiest of grounds, like a dog being a tie if they wanted to go away and a danger to the hens which they kept down the garden, but she had begged and pestered and promised that she would never go away and they could shoot the dog if it touched the hens.

They gave in; when one puppy was left in the litter produced by Flossie, the butcher's bitch, and the butcher offered it to anyone who wanted it in the meat queue on Friday morning, her mother said she could have it and brought it home with the weekend leg of lamb.

He was a terrier, black, white and brown, with a bit of mongrel thrown in. She cared about him much more than she cared about anybody else in her family. He was probably about equal with Kate.

Her mother had had to go away because somebody was ill. The boys were away at camp. Mrs Hough was to come and keep house.

'Can I have Kate to stay?' she had asked immediately. Of course her mother said yes. Her mother liked Kate.

It was on the second day that the awful thing happened. They had just gone through the little gate into the vegetable garden and were walking along the path towards the toolshed when they heard this squawking noise. In the middle of the hen run, Bisto was standing triumphant, like some conquering hero, evidently taking a breather while a dozen hens squawked and fluttered and ran all over the place. There were feathers everywhere. She'd dashed with Kate into the run. Bisto set off again chasing a large white Leghorn towards the henhouse. They grabbed him. He didn't seem to understand the awfulness of his crime; he wagged his tail, obviously pleased with himself, expecting praise.

Then they saw it. A Rhode Island Red, it was, lying on its back with its stupid yellow legs sticking up in the air.

'They'll shoot him,' she had sobbed. 'They'll put him to sleep. It's illegal to kill hens.'

'Better tell Mrs Hough,' Kate had said.

Mrs Hough was a farmer's widow. She was very fat and didn't move around much. She was sitting in the kitchen, when they went to find her, having a snack of tea with bread and dripping. She had a very big head with lots of grey hair wound in a thick plait, like a twisted sausage, round her head.

She shook the plaited sausage and pulled down the corners of her mouth.

'He'll likely do it again,' she said. 'Now he's found out how.'

'Oh, no, we'll never let him. What we want to know is what do we do now?'

'You could sell the hen and buy another to match it.'

19

Oh, brilliant Mrs Hough. Why hadn't they thought of that?

'Who'd buy it?' Kate asked. 'And where do you get new ones?'

'Leave it to Mrs Hough,' Mrs Hough said. 'And go and fetch the hen.'

It was horrible carrying the dead hen. In the end they found a spade and shovelled it into a big bucket and carried that up to Mrs Hough in the kitchen.

She had cleared away the bread and dripping and was having a snack of blackberry and apple pie.

'I'll show you what you must do,' she said, 'so he'll not kill again. Get some string and bring the dog here.'

They watched with growing horror as she tied the hen's legs together with the string. Then she attached it tightly to Bisto's collar. He backed away from the dead thing which flopped against his chest, but could not escape it.

'Twenty-four hours with that round his neck and he'll not touch another hen,' Mrs Hough said. 'Ever.'

'Oh, no, no.'

He was walking backwards, tail right down between his legs, his body all hunched up, a picture of despair and terror.

'We can't do it to him,' she said, beginning to cry.

'In the dark,' Mrs Hough said.

'The dark?' It came out as a shriek.

'Coalhouse,' Mrs Hough said.

They watched while she put Bisto, almost unrecognisable in his misery, into the coalhouse, the awful thing hanging round his neck.

'Food?' she had managed to whisper.

'Nothing to eat or drink for twenty-four hours,' Mrs Hough said.

They stood outside the door and they heard this dreadful sound. It was a kind of thin wail, hardly audible, a thread of pure misery.

'He'll not do it again,' Mrs Hough said. 'Time for your supper.'

They couldn't eat and went supperless to bed.

She didn't sleep either; at midnight she couldn't bear it any longer and, keeping to the outside of the stairs where they didn't creak, made her way down, turned the key in the back door, tugged

20

back the heavy iron bolts and let herself out into the garden. In the stillness of the night it reached her, that awful subdued howling, that thin and desolate wail, growing ever louder as she drew nearer the coalhouse.

She knew she mustn't let him out; he had to be cured. She just wanted to share his misery, be in there with him, let him know she hadn't abandoned him. As she struggled with the heavy latch, she heard a sound behind her. She looked round. The ghost was walking towards her, transparent, white. She screamed but no sound came out.

'It's me,' Kate said. 'Don't be scared.'

Kate in a white nightdress with the kitchen light shining through her.

'I thought I'd just go in with him for a while,' she said, managing to keep the wobble out of her voice. 'And I wasn't scared,' she added.

'Don't be daft. She'd know. You'd be black all over with coal.'

And Kate led her back upstairs, taking charge, bolting the doors, turning off the light. And all the time they could hear Bisto's terrified whimpering.

Kate got into bed with her and they lay in each other's arms for comfort and, just before dawn, fell asleep.

No, she hadn't just envied Kate. She had loved her too.

They must have been an odd little pair, she thought now, herself all sharp edges, Kate softer, gentler. She'd never really considered at the time whether they actually liked each other or not. Kate was there and that was all there was to it. When you're older you need to have things in common with friends, share opinions. Children don't do this – at least she didn't. She probably did have more in common with later friends at college, and work, but there would never be another friend like Kate. It wouldn't matter if they didn't see each other for years, they would still be drawn together by something which went much deeper than common interests: their shared memories.

Kate was her best friend and sometimes she hated her. But however much they quarrelled, they were always on the same side. She knew that Kate would fight alongside her if she was attacked by one of her brothers. And of course she would have killed Kate's mother for her if Kate had required her to do so.

They'd been allies against the grown-ups. You need an ally, she realised now, more than twenty years on, when you don't have the experience to deal with the adult world. You need someone whose reactions you understand because they're the same as your own, when you are up against the inexplicability of adults. She and Kate had shared all the disasters and fears.

It was Kate who noticed the blood on Bisto's jaws when he came in from one of his sorties in the village.

'Look, there, on his beard,' she said. 'It's dripping.'

They dragged him down to the garden, held him under the tap by the greenhouse, shoved his face into the water barrel for good measure, until there was no blood to be seen.

'He might have cut himself?' she had suggested hopefully.

'No,' Kate said. 'It's something else's blood.'

'He's never looked at a hen since – since, you know. And he's never worried sheep or anything like that.'

'He was coming away from the butcher's,' Kate said.

They looked at each other, both remembering the time when they had seen him emerge from the back of the butcher's shop with a piece of steak in his mouth. Kate had held the butcher in conversation while she, Betty, had crept round the back and replaced the steak on the wooden block with a lot of other meat.

'Perhaps this time he ate it first,' she suggested.

'Or killed someone else's hen,' Kate pointed out ominously. 'It's no good, we've just got to keep him with us all the time.'

They were alone in the house that afternoon, playing marbles, when the doorbell rang.

'I'll go,' she said, feeling importantly grown-up.

A large farmer with a red face and whiskers stood on the doorstep.

'Do you have a dog?' he asked.

She stared at him, horrified, remembering the blood on Bisto's jaws, remembering the Rhode Island Red.

'No,' she said. 'We don't have no dog. I mean any dogs. I mean, no, we don't.'

'Oh.' He sounded disappointed. 'I had it in mind I'd seen you with a dog.'

'No,' she said, shaking her head. 'Absolutely not,' she added for emphasis.

A muffled bark came from the kitchen. Bisto must be wondering where she'd gone. Please God, make Kate keep him out of the way. But she knew that there was no need to bother God really; she could trust Kate to be listening at the door, keeping her hand tight over Bisto's mouth.

'You see,' the farmer said, 'we need a terrier for ratting. We've got rats in some of the barns and there's nothing like a terrier for driving them out. Our dogs are no use for ratting. So I thought I might borrow yours.'

'Oh, a dog,' she said, as if suddenly remembering. 'A dog. Well, yes, of course. Yes, I remember now. We do have a dog and he's a terrier. He'd love to come with you and chase your rats, I'm sure he would. Any time.'

She was burbling with relief.

'I thought you said log,' she added for good measure.

Bisto went three times to the farm. She didn't know what he did exactly but he was very good at it and the farmer was very pleased with him. She hoped he enjoyed it; she hoped it made up for the hen.

It was an achievement, this book of Kate's, Betty thought as she got out of the bath. And Kate was married and had two children. Not bad for somebody who'd just reached thirty. What had she herself done to compare with that? she wondered, suddenly discontented. Well, quite a lot, actually, she reminded herself. And it was good that she could rejoice in Kate's success and not need to compete with her, keep up, as she had always done when they were little. She'd grown out of that sort of thing now.

She'd lain in the bath too long; her fingers were puckered at the tips. The rest of her was all right, she thought, looking critically at her dripping reflection in the full-length mirror on the bathroom wall. Those long legs, so mocked by her brothers, won admiration now. Ostrich, they used to call her, after she'd come first in all the races at school. It was intended – and taken – as an insult. Odd to think that what had once been a term of abuse was now one of praise. Only last week Colin had been extolling her wonderful legs that went on and on and finally disappeared into her armpits. It wasn't an original thought, of course, but then he wasn't a very original person, she reflected, beginning to dry first one long leg and then the other.

They were hairless, too, which saved her hours with razor, wax and tweezers and all the weaponry with which other girls went into battle with their incorrigibly fuzzy limbs. Really it was just that the hair was so fair that it didn't show, like the eyebrows of her youth, now grown darker and anyway easily emphasised with eyebrow pencil. But what agonies her unsatisfactory body had caused her at the time.

Puberty had come late; so late she'd almost given it up. Everyone seemed to be changing except her. Development they called it. It wasn't so bad when she was still at the village school but then her parents sent her away to an all-girls school where everyone else in her form was developing and she wasn't. She was the same straight up-and-down shape – or rather non-shape – that she had always been. She was quite flat. All around her, hips were widening, breasts sprouting. Menstruation was in the air. In bedroom and bathroom they chattered about boyfriends, as they slipped neat little breasts into lacy triangles of lingerie or ladled vast bosoms into great hammocks of bras, while she hid her childish body under her bath towel. Sometimes they stopped their talk as she approached, as if they were grown-ups and she was too young to be included. But she was the same age. That was what was so awful.

Compared to this abject bodily failure, being top of the class was no consolation. At the end of her first year she tried to do as badly as possible in exams in the hope of being kept down. In the form below there were six girls, admittedly nearly a year younger than she was, who were equally late in developing, still flat and pre-menstrual. She'd done her research and she knew.

It didn't work; she only succeeded in coming third instead of first, so got into trouble from the staff for not trying, but would still have to go up next September with the wide-hipped, full-breasted, menstruating mob.

It was possible, she thought as she came home for the holidays, that she might never achieve any of these things; perhaps nature had intended her to be a boy. To make matters worse, Kate wasn't coming back to Netherby this summer. Not that she could have talked to Kate about it, not really. They had always shared everything but somehow to approach the plump-breasted Kate, complete with rounded hips and periods, and consult her about this awfulness would be too humiliating. And she'd rather die than ask her mother. In the end she put a roundabout kind of question to Mrs Hough concerning animal development.

'Pigs,' Mrs Hough said, looking up from her mid-morning snack of left-over Yorkshire pudding and hotted-up gravy, followed by fruit cake, 'can be difficult. Just the odd one in a litter. We call 'em Murphies.'

'Murphies?'

'Short for Maphradites,' Mrs Hough said. 'Neither one thing nor t'other. Not worth fattening 'em up. Might as well kill 'em young,' she added as she turned back to her fruit slab.

Betty thanked her. So she was a hermaphrodite, that was it. It didn't sound very loveable. Well, she didn't care. If nobody loved her, she'd just love herself. She called Bisto and set off briskly for a long walk, head held high, defying the world, and didn't stop until she reached the top of the dale. There by the stream she sat down, Bisto alongside her, panting. It was suddenly unbearable. She put her arms around his neck and leant against him and told him all about it: the loneliness, the being different, how she would never grow up like the others, never get married, never have children. Soon she was sobbing with self-pity and the tufted, wiry hair of his chest was wet with her tears. He sat quite still, every now and then flicking out his long pink tongue to give her face a swift, casual lick.

She cried until she gave herself stomach-ache. Then she got up and set off for home, rubbing her tears away with the back of her hand, trying to ignore the cramping pain. As she came back into the village she set her face defiantly, so that nobody would know, especially not her horrible brothers, and wished she could swap the three of them for an elder sister, somebody really nice like Chrissie Newbould.

Bisto followed at her heels, tired now and less inclined to dash backwards and forwards between her and whatever caught his attention ahead. It was only when she got home that she realised she was menstruating.

'About time too,' her mother said, and saw to everything.

The breasts followed shortly afterwards. Not the floppy sort or the widespread sort, but the neat, compact little sort. Very sensitive they were too. She wouldn't, of course, have realised how much that mattered if it hadn't been for Tony.

Dear Tony, so utterly incompetent at organising his life, always in the wrong place, forgetting dates, arriving late, a hopeless muddler, never sure what direction he wanted to go in. But in bed he knew exactly what he wanted and – more important – what she wanted. Instinctively he knew it. He knew when the gentle touch must give way to the firmer touch, he knew when the hands must move on and where, he knew how far, how deep. Instinctively he knew these things and instinctively she responded like a dancing partner. It was lovely and she grew up thanks to Tony; it was he who transformed her from girl to woman. He wasn't, of course, the sort of man you could possibly marry, he would never achieve anything in life, dear disorganised thing that he was. He was strictly for bedtime.

Her tutor, Lionel, was, by contrast, an authoritative man, immensely capable, very well organised. Maybe that was what had appealed to her after the chaotic Tony. She could go out with Lionel knowing that everything would go smoothly, it was very relaxing. He just took over and saw to everything. But in bed he was anything but authoritative: he was indecisive; his hands darted about. It was horrible. Just as one of her sensitive breasts responded to his touch, his hands would rush off somewhere else. And even if they didn't, she couldn't relax because she thought that they might.

She had really liked him as a man, that was what was so infuriating. She'd tried to explain to him. After all one should always try to talk, or rather talk things *through*, as the experts put it. So she'd tried to explain about the vulnerability. No wonder some women could never really abandon themselves to sex when there were men like Lionel about, she had thought to herself, as she tried to explain to him that you have to feel safe, confident in your man, trust him, before you can surrender to passion. He didn't even bother to file his nails properly, she thought, shivering with remembered horror and frustration. He had put her off sex for a time, Lionel had.

Quite a short time, actually, because then there was Miles.

Miles was another contrast. He really was a swine, insensitive, a maker of snide remarks. She'd taken an instant dislike to him – until he kissed her. After that their affair moved swiftly. And this same insensitive Miles was the most sensitive of lovers, considerate and endlessly inventive. Yes, inventive, this unimaginative man.

Yet the experts on these matters, the writers of books on

psychology, the counsellors, the knowing ones, always said that a person's sexual nature was part and parcel of their general personality. It sounded logical; it was just that it wasn't true. Of course most of the writers were men so they couldn't know, could they? she'd thought. They had only their own experience to go on, they didn't really know about other men. Not the way that women do. And they couldn't really know themselves as an outsider would, as a woman would. No wonder they got it wrong.

What about women? she asked herself, carefully drying between her toes. Not too difficult to be honest about your sexual character, she thought, but impossible to be impartial about your whole personality. In both spheres, she thought, trying to do the impossible, she was herself calculating. She was more giving, though, more eager to please, in bed than she was at work. Certainly more happy to surrender, to lose control. In other areas of life she liked to be in charge.

Colin was about the only man she'd known of whom she would have said that his sexual nature and character coincided. He was calculating too, of course, in both spheres. They understood that about each other. They got on well in bed and elsewhere. And he was very appreciative, she thought, as she finished drying and began rubbing cream into her long legs, down her arms, across her breasts and stomach.

She sighed as she looked at herself in the glass. It was a lovely body, pale and slender, which had developed out of that childish angularity. She stretched her arms above her head so that the long legs really did seem to extend into her armpits, the line of them tapering along her arms right up to the tips of her fingers. Her hips were narrow still, her waist small, her breasts pointed and high.

It was an unused body, she thought suddenly. Childless. She would have to move fast if she was to keep up with Kate in the marriage and fertility stakes.

She took the big powder puff and began smoothing talc all over her body. If Colin's purpose in asking her out to this candlelit dinner was to propose marriage to her, she might be well-advised to accept.

27

Chapter Three

'Oh, Chrissie, I forgot to tell you,' Jack said, getting into bed. 'I saw Luke today and he told me Kate's written a book about their time in Sri Lanka.'

'Goodness, will we be in it?'

He laughed. 'It's about the place, not us.'

He reached for his wallet on the bedside table and took out a slip of paper.

'Here are the details,' he said. 'You can get it, can't you? Oh, and could you order it from the library as well?'

She was nursing full-time at the hospital now, but it was still taken for granted that the buying of books, like the buying of meat and vegetables, was her responsibility.

'But we shan't need it from the library if I've bought it,' she pointed out, sitting down at the dressing-table and reaching for her hairbrush.

'No, but it's good for the book trade apparently.'

He yawned and stretched.

'You know, Chrissie,' he went on, abruptly changing the subject as he leant back against the pillows, 'the Eighties are going to be a wonderful time. And nobody seems to realise it, they just haven't grasped what it will be like, being an oil state.'

'Ninety-nine, one hundred,' Chrissie murmured and put down the hairbrush.

She had been eighteen when he married her, but she still kept up the nightly routine of brushing her hair a hundred times. He watched as she scraped the comb through the brush, dropped the resultant little ball of hair into the wastepaper basket and climbed into bed beside him.

'Well, it's hard to imagine, Jack. I mean, oil states have always been in hot places, haven't they? With sand and Arabs and things like that. Not here, not in places like Britain. That's why

29

people can't really take it in. I mean ordinary people, not people like you.'

She saw the smile and added, 'You know what I mean, it's different for civil engineers. It's part of your work.'

'We were looking at the figures today,' he said, slipping his arms under and around her. 'We'll soon be a net exporter of oil. Think of it, after all these years of struggling to pay our way in the world, we need never have a balance of payments crisis again.'

She was tired; she had other things on her mind than the balance of payments. Things like Claire's exams and Sarah's boyfriend. And now she mustn't forget to get this book of Kate's. Dear Kate, it had been lovely having her out in Sri Lanka when the men were working together. And Daniel was a darling and her only godson. She hoped for Kate's sake that he would have an easier adolescence than Claire seemed to be having, but maybe daughters are more difficult for mothers to understand, she said to herself. I mean you wouldn't expect a boy to be like yourself, would you?

'And think of the tax revenue there'll be,' Jack was saying. She knew he was wide-awake and needed to mull over the events of the day, so she put her worries about Claire out of her mind and snuggled up against him, having first taken his right hand and placed it on the side of her breast, exactly where she best liked it to be, and prepared to listen.

'They reckon about four billion pounds next year, and soon rising to ten or twelve billion per annum,' he was saying. 'Just think what you can do with that – it's a huge, unexpected bonus. It's a lucky government that's in power in the Eighties.'

'What will they spend it on?' she prompted, moving his hand to the other side and closing her eyes.

'Oh, the whole infrastructure. We waste a third of our water through leaky pipes. The Victorians made a good job of laying them, but they need replacing now. I'd do that first. Then of course, transport. We'll be able to have the best railway system in Europe by the end of the decade.'

He heard her yawn.

'I'm sorry, Chrissie,' he said. 'You're tired. What sort of day have you had?'

She thought about it. 'Busy,' was all she could say. She didn't analyse things the way he did. Behind her tired eyelids hospital scenes rolled; trolleys trundled down corridors, beds were pushed about, patients in worn dressing gowns shuffled across wards.

'Couldn't some of the money go on the health service, Jack?' she requested.

He put the other arm round her and drew her close, stroking back the hair from her face. It had been a great halo of gold when he first kissed her, all those years ago, framing a serenely beautiful face. Time had dulled it now with flecks of grey and the face, twenty-four years and two children later, was more careworn but lovely still. To Jack, workaholic though he was, she was still the best, the truest, the most precious thing in his life. And still the most exciting.

'There should be enough by the mid-Eighties to get rid of all the hospital waiting lists,' he assured her and having thus granted his wife several billion pounds, he drew her closer to him and began, in his leisurely way, to kiss the closed lids and seek out all the warm, familiar places.

'Of course, it was different in your day, Mum,' Claire said, moving her books to make room for the coffee. 'Thanks. I mean, women saw themselves differently. They had a different conception of themselves.'

Chrissie tried to remember ever having had a conception of herself. She failed.

'In your day you just saw yourself as an adjunct of some man.'

Chrissie wasn't absolutely sure what an adjunct was, nor who was meant by 'some man'. As far as men went, there had been her father and then there'd been Jack.

'Of course it wasn't your fault,' Claire conceded. 'I'm not saying that for one moment. In fact it was very hard for you.'

Chrissie nodded. She remembered falling in love with Jack and it had been lovely.

'I mean the pill wasn't invented and then sex was so different.'
'Was it?'

Her daughter gave a little laugh and then smiled at her mother, shaking her head as if in disbelief at her ignorance.

'But of course it was,' she told her, as confidently as if she'd actually been there at the time. 'I mean before Germaine Greer

31

invented the clitoris, women had no pleasure. They just gave in to their man's demands. Sex was a man's pleasure.'

'Was it?'

'And those poor women had a dreadful time on their honeymoon. No pleasure at all.'

Chrissie remembered going away with Jack after their wedding. The bliss of being on their own at last. The days and nights in bed, just loving each other after all the waiting and all those partings, the self-forgetfulness of it, the abandon, the long drawn-out satisfaction, the wonder of it, the surprise. Pleasure did seem rather a weak and inadequate word for all that.

'That's what the books say, is it?' she queried.

'Oh, Mum, it's not just in the books. It's common knowledge. Our generation are so lucky, we do realise that. We are the first women to have real sexual freedom. We're just very privileged that we live in the Age of the Orgasm.'

It sounded to Chrissie rather threatening, a bit like a thunderstorm. So she just smiled and picked up the empty cup.

'Why doesn't Dad do the ironing?' her daughter demanded suddenly.

'The ironing?' her mother repeated, surprised. 'It's done. It's Thursday. Why, do you have something needs to be pressed?'

'No. It's the principle of the thing. He just ought to do it.'

'I'm sure he's quite able to do it, but he's never been at home when it needed doing, you see,' she explained. 'It was just more sensible for me to do it while I was at home anyway looking after you.'

It was odd that this clever daughter of hers hadn't understood an obvious thing like that, she couldn't help thinking. Claire looked at her and shook her head.

'It's probably too late to change you now,' she said resignedly.

'Will you be applying to deliver the Christmas mail this year?' Chrissie asked to cheer her up.

'Oh yes. Can you get me a form? I loved it last year and I made all that money.'

This was safer ground. This was more like the old Claire.

'It means getting up very early,' she pointed out.

'I don't mind.'

Claire thought for a moment and then went on, 'You know what I really did mind, Mum?'

32

'No. What was that?'

'The way some people got no post at all. Some houses had dozens and dozens of cards and then there were others that got nothing except just a bill now and then, even at Christmas.'

'I remember.'

She remembered Claire coming home almost in tears about it. She leant over her and for a moment Claire rested her head gently against her mother's breast for comfort.

Then, 'Mum, have you finished the curtains for my room yet?' she asked.

'Nearly. I've got to go off to work now, but I'll finish them tomorrow and we'll take them back with you to college next week and hang them up for you.'

'Thanks, Mum. You're great.'

Chapter Four

Claire sat at her desk in the top floor room of the terrace house in North Oxford which she shared with four other students, and thought about her parents. She had been at the university for two terms now, reading psychology, and had come to realise what a boring sort of family she had, who did such predictable things.

The others had far more interesting parents; Ginny's mother had left home and set up house with a lesbian friend and written a book about it. Simone had a French mother who lived with an Italian student half her age. Jerry's parents moved about the world arranging exhibitions and Milo didn't even know who his parents were.

Claire felt very left out when they sat in the kitchen discussing their parents' marital affairs, or more usually their extra-marital ones, when all she could offer was a mother who was a farmer's daughter who had married a civil engineer when she was eighteen and taken up nursing late in life. And now they were moving to Staines, of all places. Needless to say, neither of her parents had ever run off with anybody.

There was Aunt Nell, of course. That was something on the credit side. Nell was her mother's cousin, an academic who had lived for years with a writer. Not that her mother acknowledged this; she always referred to her cousin's lover as 'Nell's friend Mr Nansen'. But Claire had discussed it all, of course, with her elder sister, Sarah, and they had agreed long ago that their mother really thought that Aunt Nell was living in sin.

In the same way, their parents managed not to perceive Sarah's relationship with her boyfriend. If he came to stay they gave him his own bedroom for all the world as if he and Sarah weren't living together in Potters Bar.

'It's ridiculous,' Claire had objected to Sarah after he had left last time. 'I don't know why you put up with it.'

Sarah had only shrugged. 'What does it matter?' she asked. 'It's no trouble to go and rumple up the spare bed in the morning.'

'But it's so, so, oh, I don't know, it's so hypocritical.'

'So what? Hypocrisy is only the homage which vice pays to virtue.'

Claire had been impressed, not realising that it was a quotation.

It suddenly occurred to her now that perhaps Sarah and Ian were going to get married. Why else should her sister have rung last night and said she had something important to talk about and would come over in time for lunch? What else was there that couldn't be discussed on the phone? The more she thought about it the more it seemed horribly possible that Sarah was going to desert to the other side, turn all conventional and want to dress up in virginal white and expect her, Claire, to be a bridesmaid in frills.

The parents would be pleased; they'd be really relieved that at least one of their daughters wasn't going to turn out like Aunt Nell – clever, different, unconventional. Not, to be fair, that her mother ever criticised, much less condemned. They were solid old things, she thought tolerantly as she turned back to her notes for an essay on The Sexual Mores of the Single Woman in the Post-Industrial Society. They were always there, unchanging, boring, stuck in some kind of time-warp. If only they would just for once do something interesting, something surprising.

'I went home last weekend and there's something Mum wants to talk to you about,' Sarah said, as they sat by the gas fire in Claire's room drinking coffee and eating the pizza which Sarah had brought with her. 'But she didn't want to do it on the phone and can't come here herself so we thought the best thing was for me to come and see you.'

Panic. Her mother was ill. Please God, not cancer. I can't bear it if she dies. She's always been there. I love her more than anyone in the world. She stared at her sister, white-faced.

'Oh, Sarah,' she managed to whisper. 'Is she going to die?'

'Honestly! You just let that imagination of yours run riot, don't you? No, of course she's not ill.'

'Then what?' Sarah asked, still in a whisper.

'She's pregnant.'

36

'Pregnant?' Her voice came out in a shriek this time. 'She can't be. Not at her age.'

'It's not unknown for women in their forties to have babies.'

'But it's not as if she's been having them for years like women used to. I mean she hasn't had any since us.'

'She had a miscarriage.'

'But to be having a baby at forty-two! It'll seem so ridiculous. I mean I just can't think of anyone else it's happened to. She'll look so conspicuous.'

'Rubbish,' her sister told her sharply. 'It's marvellous and she and Dad are absolutely thrilled about it. They've known for a few months now.'

'And never told us?'

'I expect they had their reasons.'

'She didn't look pregnant at Christmas.'

'Well, she does now. She's only got four months to go.'

Claire did a quick calculation. 'Then they must have done it in October,' she said. 'When they went to Scotland, after leaving me here.'

'You make it sound like a plot. I promise you it was all unplanned.'

It was true; she did feel plotted against. They'd dropped her off here and gone off to Scotland and conceived this baby. It was unbelievable, apart from the thought of her parents actually coupling at their age – yuk!

'A few moments ago you were in a panic in case she was going to die,' Sarah cut in. 'And now you haven't even asked if she's well.'

'I was just going to,' Claire said humbly.

'She's fine. She looks blooming. You'll see for yourself at Easter.'

'It's going to be so embarrassing. I mean us grown up and her pregnant. Our own mother!'

She pictured herself leading her mother into the kitchen, introducing her to the others, to Ginny and Simone, Jerry and Milo. She shuddered.

'And embarrassing for Dad too,' she added.

'He's as proud as can be of her – and so should you be,' Sarah told her and there was anger in her voice.

'Yes, I'm sorry. I mean I am really. It's just that it takes a bit of getting used to.'

It's always like this, she thought miserably; I always know how I should feel, but I never manage to feel it. Something gets in the way and fights against it. Oh, why do I get into such muddles? She knew she had no right to feel outrage at her parents' extraordinary behaviour, but she did. Why couldn't she be more like calm and sensible Sarah with her steady teaching job? She herself had no idea what she wanted to do when she left college.

'How is Ian?' she asked politely. 'Any news about the two of you?'

'Oh, we've split up,' Sarah said. 'He'll be moving into the new flat by himself. I quite forgot to tell you in all this. But whatever's wrong? Claire, don't look like that.'

Claire's eyes had filled with tears.

'I thought the news was going to be that you were getting married,' she said. 'And now I wish it had been. Isn't it ridiculous?'

She collapsed suddenly in a giggling fit and her sister looked at her despairingly and wished to God she'd grow up.

Two things astonished Claire when Rosemary was born. The first was Rosemary herself. She hadn't had anything to do with a baby before and was nonplussed by the smallness of it. She couldn't stop gazing at this amazing creature, this miniature thing with its tiny hands and mottled, washer-woman arms no bigger than a doll's. Matching feet too, she observed with further astonishment, toes like minute shrimps, pink and crinkled.

Her mother didn't seem to share this wonder and that was the other astonishing thing. In fact her mother was down-to-earth and practical, not overwhelmed at all.

'She'll have to give up work of course,' Claire had remarked to Sarah before the baby was born.

'No, she'll have maternity leave and then go back to the hospital.'

'But who'll look after the baby?'

'She'll make a good arrangement, don't worry.'

'But it's not like Mum to do that, she never worked when we were little. I mean she was always there when we came in from school and—'

'Honestly, Claire, you really are the limit. How many times have you said women shouldn't be tied by children? All this women's rights stuff you're on about and when it's your own mother—'

'Well, it's different when it's your own mother.'

She thought about it, wanting to rationalise this very strong feeling she had, this need to defend the baby's rights.

'Mum's generation of women stayed at home with their children,' she explained. 'That's how it was in their day. It just doesn't seem natural for her to behave like this.'

'Look, Claire, it isn't just a matter of people changing, it's the times which have changed. Mum belongs to the nineteen-eighties just as much as you or me or anyone else. She waited to take up nursing for years and she's trained now and I think she's quite right not to give it up. Why should there be different rules for her just because she's forty-two?'

Claire was just going to say that that was the whole trouble, having babies at forty-two, but she held the words back, not wanting to risk further sisterly wrath.

And of course her mother did make a good arrangement. Mrs Rawley, who lived on the housing estate on the other side of the roundabout, whose husband was a porter at the hospital, came in each day and looked after Rosemary. And Chrissie went back to work and seemed to shed ten years so that, when she and Claire went out with the pram together, nobody mistook Chrissie for the baby's grandmother as Claire had feared they might.

•

Chapter Five

'I thought we might ask a few friends in to celebrate,' Kate said. 'Well, not exactly celebrate, but just have dinner to mark the occasion.'

'What occasion?' Luke asked, not looking up from his paper.

'My novel coming out.'

'Oh, that.'

'Well, perhaps it wasn't such a good idea,' she said, deflated. 'After all, we didn't do anything special when the travel book came out last year. Of course, I did have that lovely peaceful walk up at Netherby,' she added hastily, not wanting to sound ungrateful. 'And you cooked a wonderful candlelit dinner, but I mean we didn't invite anybody round, did we?'

He put the paper down. 'Come here,' he said and kissed her. 'Of course we must celebrate. You go ahead and arrange it. Who would you like to ask?'

'I'm sure Jack and Chrissie could come,' she said, settling herself comfortably on his knee. 'You know, the great compensation for me when you told me we were moving south was that we'd be nearer Chrissie and Jack?'

'Did you mind so very much? Leaving Yorkshire, I mean?'

She thought about it.

'Well, yes I did. But I'd always known it was a bit of luck having that time there. And I always knew we'd be nomads,' she said. 'And it's more convenient to like where you have to be.'

'That sounds a bit grudging.'

'No, because then I was surprised at how quickly I felt at home here. Wiltshire is like Yorkshire, in a way. Up on the Ridgeway it feels like home. It's something to do with the wildness of it, the timelessness.'

She thought of the great sweep of those ancient hills, the way the shadows rushed across them on a blustery day on White Horse

41

Hill, when the children flew kites and their cheeks glowed from the wind and sun.

'From a practical point of view,' Luke was saying, 'we'll be more settled now that I'm setting up the regional office here.'

'You don't mind that? You don't miss being on site?'

He shrugged.

'It's like you said just now. It's more convenient to like what has to be. And I shall still get around the sites, of course I shall. Jack's had to adjust to being in head office after working on site in Scotland. But come on, who else will you ask to this dinner party?'

'Nell, if she's still staying with them.'

'Remind me about Nell.'

'She's Chrissie's cousin. She was brought up with her in Netherby. I think she was an orphan. I don't really know – Betty and I were much younger than they were. Anyway she and Chrissie are very close, but so different in character,' she added thoughtfully.

'How do you mean?'

'She was always a much spikier person than Chrissie. She's very clever and unconventional. She's an economist, I think, anyway something like that. She's at Wincleriton University. I like her, she's a bit of a dark horse and you never quite know what she'll say next.'

'And who else will you ask?'

'I thought I'd ask Betty and Colin.'

'But they live in London, don't they?'

'Yes. I suppose it's a bit of a long way to expect them to come just for dinner. But I bet Colin's got an enormously expensive fast car.'

Luke laughed.

'What makes you think that?'

'Oh, I just get the impression he's very rich. He's gone into the City and does great financial deals,' she added vaguely. 'Currency dealings, pushing money around, and all that. But I'd love to see Betty again. We've talked a lot on the phone since we've been in touch, but we haven't managed to meet.'

'Wasn't theirs the wedding we couldn't go to?'

'Yes, we were in the middle of moving. It was a shame we couldn't make it. Apparently it was terribly grand.'

'Not like ours,' Luke said.

He held her close as they both remembered the wedding in the dingy little registry office, the same one to which she had so recently gone to register her father's death.

'Do you mind?' he asked gently. 'I mean do you sometimes wish you could look back on the sort of wedding most girls have? I don't mean grand like Betty's, but just a bit more romantic than ours.'

She shook her head.

'No, I don't mind at all,' she said. 'It was the best we could do at the time. And anyway it's what comes afterwards that matters.'

'And that's been all right?' he asked anxiously.

'You know it has.'

They lay holding each other close in the big, shabby old armchair, contented with their lot.

'Have you thought of a date? For the dinner party, I mean,' he said at last.

'Publication day's a fortnight on Thursday.'

He took his diary out of his pocket.

'No good. It's election night.'

'Does that matter?'

'Some people like to sit up all night watching the results come in. I'd rather they didn't do it here. Too busy the next day.'

'All right. And, come to think of it, Betty said Colin had political ambitions so he's probably doing something special that night. We could make it the previous Friday.'

'That's all right by me. If you're sure you can manage.'

He was being tactful, remembering other dinner parties. She attempted a reassuring smile. She knew she would never be really domesticated. It didn't come naturally to her as it seemed to do to other women. Tasks which they hardly seemed aware of doing, became immensely complicated when she set about them. Just peeling a few vegetables seemed to cause chaos in her kitchen. It wasn't that she disliked cooking. In fact she found it relaxing after sitting for hours writing at her desk. She enjoyed making a complicated dish so long as nobody minded when it was ready or expected to eat anything much before or after it. It was just the organising that she was bad at, the getting of everything ready at the same time. It was all right for the family, but dinner parties verged on the chaotic.

'Chrissie was telling me that it's just a question of doing as much as possible well in advance,' she told her husband now, to allay his anxiety. 'I'll really try to do that this time.'

Chrissie was always so calm; where Chrissie was, order prevailed. She never seemed hurried; things just seemed to get done on time. Kate presumed it was some kind of knack, maybe something bred into her from infancy, from watching her mother in the farm kitchen. She herself had never had the chance to pick up any such skills at home as a child. And at school she hadn't learned to cook because she'd taken Latin, and there seemed to be an assumption that one had to choose between the two, as if classicists didn't need to eat. In Sri Lanka, a local boy, called Nirad, had been in charge of the kitchen. He wasn't a great cook; mostly he gave them a mixture of the contents of imported tins followed by such local delicacies as curd and kittul. She hadn't interfered, partly because she didn't want to upset him and partly because she knew she couldn't do any better herself.

She'd learned more about gardening than cooking from Nirad, who had taken over the plot of land at the back of the bungalow and turned it into a garden. Here he grew all their vegetables, serving up, day after day, bowlfuls of any that were in season. Back home, she had done likewise, particularly now that they'd moved from Yorkshire to Wiltshire, to a house with a much bigger garden.

The house, Kate reflected as she did some unaccustomed dusting and hoovering in preparation for the guests, did perhaps look a bit neglected. It had proved impossible to write books as well as look after the family and manage both house and garden. Fortunately she had discovered, only last year, that dusting was unnecessary; so long as you didn't do any, it didn't show. The main thing was not to do just a little dusting, because that made the undusted bits show up horribly. But the garden, oh, the garden, that was a different matter entirely. It really did look loved.

She stood by the french windows, the dusting abandoned, gazing out. It was a perfect morning; after a cold night, morning dew sparkled on the grass and on the leaves. Everything looked fresh and clean, but with the promise of heat. The west-facing herbaceous bed was still in deep shade, some flower petals still furled, others just beginning to open up, waiting to be visited by the sun. The rose bed on the opposite side was brilliant in the sunshine, the soil already drier, paler.

Everything was phenomenally early this year, she realised, presumably the result of a mild winter and very early spring. And of course the garden was very sheltered; she reckoned everything in it was about a month ahead of things in her northern garden. The climbers she had planted on the old brick wall at the back of the rose bed were already coming into flower, the Albertine holding up little pale pink buds like stubby candles, while behind it, just visible, the magnolia was a mass of deeper red chalices. The philadelphus in the far corner was blossoming early because she had forgotten to prune it last year.

Normally, at this time of day, she was at her desk working immediately the children were off to school and had to resist the call of the garden, but to resist it for dusting would be positively sinful, she thought, as she left the duster on the bookcase and made for the garden.

The air was sharper than she expected, fresh against her cheeks. She wandered into the vegetable garden, giving herself the excuse of choosing this evening's vegetables. The new potatoes must be almost ready, she thought, as she went to get a fork. First picking tonight. The soil was dry, the potatoes came out easily, skeins of them attached to the haulm. She pulled it out and began digging round the plant, coming up with more and more, lying gleaming like precious nuggets in the fertile soil.

There were rows of carrots, feathery-leaved, time to thin them out. The thinnings would make lovely baby carrots for supper. She began tackling them, but stopped herself: fresh vegetables must be really fresh. She had come to think it immoral to pick them more than half an hour before they went into the pan. Ridiculous really because in the shops they called them fresh when they must be two or three days old. Ah, but the taste.

She looked at the rows of spinach; spinach soup she was giving them tonight. Flavoured with borage, which grew alongside. Plenty of lettuce and radishes for a side salad. She couldn't very well give them spinach as a vegetable as well as soup. She'd give them the first picking of beans, very small. And last year's courgettes, onions and tomatoes were in the freezer in the form of ratatouille.

On the high southern wall of the vegetable garden she had trained three pear trees. She walked alongside them now, naming

45

them: Conference, Williams, Doyenne du Commice. They reached out their long espalier arms to touch each other, their neat branches laden with tiny fruit, green and polished, like miniature waxen imitations of themselves. The plum trees, less amenable to training, straggled messily alongside. A fan was not the first shape that sprang to mind to describe them, she thought, just a twiggy cat's cradle really. The apple trees were better. Still, whatever their shape they would provide tonight's pudding. The freezer was still stacked high with last year's poached pears, sliced apples, frozen plums. And the raspberries, she remembered suddenly, they must eat all the raspberries in the freezer to make way for this year's crop.

She should really be making the casserole, she thought, but it was just the right weather for hoeing. She glanced at her watch. There was time to hoe between the roses and among the plants in the herbaceous bed. Then the weeds would all shrivel in the midday sun. It was wicked to waste such ideal hoeing weather on making casseroles.

Her other gardening mentor, after Nirad, had been old Thwaite. He had come to offer his services soon after they moved in. A powerful old man still, at well over seventy, possessed of one tooth and a vast knowledge of gardening lore that included the ancient custom of using the contents of chamber pots to water the grass and all other nitrogen-loving plants. 'Diluted of course, missus,' he always added, in case she should try it. 'Otherwise it burns. Of course,' he would add sadly, 'you don't get the supplies like you used to, not with all this indoor sanitation they have nowadays.'

For two hours each week he had taught her how to dig and hoe, plant and cut, prune and mow and trim edges. They had uprooted old shrubberies and levelled lawns. They had built bonfires together and made compost heaps. Thus she had mastered the art of turning vegetable matter into an earthy heap, friable as fruit cake. Visitors were often surprised when she led them not to the rose bed or even the vegetable plot but to the compost heap down there at the bottom of the garden.

She was just leaving the rose garden for the herbaceous border when she noticed them: the greenfly. Already. Old Thwaite didn't believe in chemical death, so she'd better spray them now when he wasn't around to look disapproving. She'd do it after the herbaceous bed. Then she really would go inside and cook. But in the herbaceous bed she noticed the gobs of cuckoo spit on the lavender bush and had to deal with that first, picking each by hand, locating the bright green crawly thing in the midst of the white foam and squashing it between finger and thumb.

So the morning slipped by, the sun journeying imperceptibly across the sky as she moved beween potting shed and border, rose bed and toolshed, trailing the hoe and the rake, carrying spray gun and watering can, until she suddenly saw that it was nearly time for the children to finish school. Just time to scrub her hands, change into more respectable trousers and sprint off to the village to collect them.

'You've got dirty nails. Expect you've been gardening,' Paulette said in that special, supercilious tone she reserved for maternal horticulture.

'And you're late,' Daniel accused.

'I'm not the last,' she pointed out, adding meanly, 'Mrs Roberts isn't here yet.'

'You are the penultimate mother,' Daniel opined.

To make up to them, she promised a visit to Mrs Scratchit's shop on the way home, although she knew it would waste precious time.

'It's my favourite place, Mrs Scratchit's,' Paulette said, mollified. 'It has *everything* in it.'

'Can I buy a mousetrap?'

'I don't expect they sell mousetraps, Daniel.'

'I heard Dad say they sold mousetraps and other sweetmeats.' Kate laughed.

'I think that was a joke, darling.'

Daniel considered, then, 'I don't think it's very funny,' he said. 'And I need a mousetrap so that if we get a mouse I can catch it for you. With cheese.'

'She sells cheese. I've seen it,' Paulette put in. 'At the back, behind the magazines.'

'Dad shouldn't say things that aren't true.'

Sweets and newspapers were the mainstay of Mrs Scratchit's shop but over the years she had added garden gnomes and fly papers, tin trays and packets of seeds, jam and dusters – and much else besides – to her stock. Children swarmed in after school to assess the display on the sweet counter, conveniently placed at their eye level, and relate it to the coppers they held in their hands. Seven or eight of them were lined up debating the merits of the contents of the glass jars as Kate took the chidren into the shop.

Behind that counter Mrs Scratchit presided and was never seen anywhere else. She was a tall, angular woman of indeterminate age. Her hair was dyed black and sculpted into an elaborate edifice created in the bouffant years of the sixties and maintained now with frequent applications of lacquer. It reminded Kate of a model of St Paul's Cathedral fashioned in candy floss which she had seen years ago on a visit to Blackpool; it had looked so solid that she couldn't believe it was made of spun sugar; Mrs Scratchit's coiffure looked so rocklike that it was hard to believe it was actually made of strands of hair.

Under this elaborate dome, the face was very white, heavily chalked with powder, but the lines on it were clearly if lightly marked, as if etched by a bird walking delicately across its icing sugar surface. Mrs Scratchit's eyes were dark brown, shrewd and watchful, and never looked away from the childen even as she talked to Kate: thirty years in the shop had taught her how swiftly small hands can transfer a Mars Bar from counter to pocket.

Her voice was high-pitched and querulous. It was also incessant. Over the years she had perfected the art of directing a monologue to the adults in the shop while simultaneously dealing with the children.

'Yes,' she said to Kate, while Daniel and Paulette inspected the sweet jars, 'we're thinking of giving up, Mr Scratchit and me. It's this VAT that's got us down. Six years we've had of it now. Six years too many if you ask me. People think we keep it, you know, but we don't, we have to charge it and hand it over to the government. Those liquorice torpedoes are tuppence for six, sonny, and all in our own time too. Unpaid tax collectors, that's all we are. It's all right for the big shops, nothing to them, with their accountants. Ten pence that bar is, sonny, it used to be called a sixpenny bar in the old days, and that was six *real* pennies. Yes, sixpenny and shilling bars they were always called until they changed everything and now nobody knows what anything should cost. As I said to Mr Scratchit last night, here we are, open from eight until six, me in here all day and him doing the deliveries and no time to do all that paper work except at night and if you make a mistake, it's prison, oh yes, they wouldn't hesitate. Those chocolate buttons are ten pence an ounce, dearie, and they say they're on the side of small businesses and they're putting us all out of business and the only small businesses are the ones that used to be big ones. No, *ten* pence, I said, and you've only got *eight* pence there. You need another *two* pence. Well, you'd better choose something else then or go shares with someone else who hasn't enough either. The liquorice coils are eight pence. And now we've heard they're going to put VAT up again. The other lot brought it down from ten per cent to eight which was better for the customers, of course, but much more difficult to work out if you haven't got the machines to do the calculations. I don't expect it bothers Sainsbury's. That's six pence for what Daniel's got and six pence for his sister's, twelve pence altogether which would have been half-a-crown in the proper old money and is daylight robbery if you ask me. But still I've voted Conservative all my life, so I just blame the blacks.'

The children grumbled all the way home, as she tried to hurry them along to make up for time lost in Mrs Scratchit's shop. Paulette tripped, fell and howled. Daniel had no doubt whose fault it was. Once home she bought favour again by giving them their favourite, baked beans, for supper.

While they ate she chopped onions, fried meat, hurled in spices and prayed that the guests would talk long enough over drinks for the casserole to cook until it was edible. Then she set off down the garden.

The soil was harder now; carrots came up unwillingly, their roots twisted round each other. The beans were really too young and took for ever to pick. A lot of the radishes had holes in them and there was whitefly on the lettuces. As she ran the muddy potatoes and carrots under the outside tap, rinsed off whitefly, pulled off stalks, she found herself thinking enviously of the joys of frozen peas, of carrots in packets of clean cellophane, of bags of ready-scrubbed potatoes. Dismissing such treacherous thoughts, she hurried indoors to scrub and peel, top and tail.

'How's it going?' Luke asked anxiously, coming into the kitchen.

'Frantic. Casserole went into the oven too late, I forgot to take the fruit out of the freezer until just now. I did take out what I thought was ratatouille this morning but when it began to thaw I saw it was rhubarb. The label had come off. And, oh God, I've just realised—'

'What is it?'

49

'The soup's still growing in the garden.'

Daniel and Paulette watched the guests arrive from a vantage point on the landing. As Jack, Chrissie and Nell took off their coats, Paulette gazed solemnly down at them, her face framed by the rails.

'Isn't there a lovely smell?' she called down. 'It's your dinner. Mummy was so busy cooking it, she could only give us a few beans on toast,' she added pathetically.

Jack looked up at her.

'Weren't you lucky?' he said. 'Baked beans are my favourite.'

Nonplussed, Paulette continued to gaze in silence until her brother put in, 'Well, we didn't leave you any.'

'Thanks, Jack, just the right reply,' Luke said, leading them into the drawing room. 'Kate's a bit busy in the kitchen, but she'll be here in a moment,' he added optimistically, having just seen her running up from the garden spilling spinach out of a trug as she ran. 'Now into bed you two,' he called back over his shoulder.

'Mummy said we could stay up until everyone had come.'

'All right, if that's what she said.'

'She did. And you shouldn't break promises.'

Colin and Betty were late, but the children still kept their vigil on the landing.

'I hope you wiped your feet,' Daniel called down to them. 'Mummy gets really cross if we come in all muddy. Sometimes we have to take our shoes right off.'

'I washed my shoes in the car,' Betty told him, extending one elegant foot. 'Want to look?'

The children shrieked and ran into their bedrooms.

'The Lies They Tell About Maggie,' Daniel called out.

'What was that about?' Jack asked as they settled with drinks in the drawing room.

'The school's organised mock elections and they had the Conservative candidate yesterday,' Kate explained, wiping her hands on her apron as she came in from the kitchen. 'She distributed copies of one of the papers which had this article called something like The Lies They Tell About Maggie.'

'I didn't see that. What sort of lies?'

'It's here,' Kate said, rummaging on the long stool which was heaped up with books and old papers.

'Lie number one is that people say she'll increase VAT and number two that she'll double prescription charges from twenty to forty pence,' she read out. 'Oh, and she'll sell off priceless national assets like BP.'

'It's monstrous to say such things,' Colin said. 'This really is a very dirty election.'

'Well,' Nell told him, 'I don't think they are lying, whoever they are. I think she is.'

Colin was outraged; he had been busy canvassing on behalf of his local candidate all week and really could have done without coming here tonight. Furthermore he was surprised that a friend of Betty's should have come in wearing a pinafore when she welcomed her guests. And there was a dirty duster on the bookshelves. And now they were casting aspersions on his leader. He could hardly bring himself to be polite. 'I have myself heard her say many times that there's no need to increase VAT,' he insisted.

'It's a simple deduction really,' Nell told him. 'She's said she's going to cut income tax and the only way she can do it is by raising VAT. She's got to get the money from somewhere.'

Kate listened apprehensively; her anxiety about the casserole now replaced by anxiety that the guests might start quarrelling. Perhaps it was a mistake to invite an economist and an ambitious politician to the same meal.

'Let's ban the election,' Betty said, unabashed. 'We've all had enough of it already. The topic's banned. Agreed?'

'Agreed,' Jack said. 'And it doesn't really matter who gets in anyway. Both parties have the means of investing so much in the infrastructure now. Even politicians can't make a mess of the Eighties. Sorry, Colin,' he added, 'I hear you'd like to be one.'

If Colin was annoyed, he managed not to show it. He had remembered the advice he had been given that a candidate must never show annoyance to the electorate. Never risk losing a vote. So he must just think of his hosts and fellow-guests as electors, to be charmed and pleased and flattered. To be taken into his confidence.

'Frankly,' he said, 'I'm not at all proud of the performance of my party in the Seventies. It'll be different next time, I can promise you. We'll do the very opposite, or I'll know the reason why.'

He hadn't so much forgotten his support of those policies,

51

as obliterated it from his mind. If you're going to convince the electorate, he had come to realise, you must first convince yourself. As far as he was concerned, it simply hadn't happened, the three-day week and all that.

'Banned,' Betty reminded him and they all laughed and the conversation turned to other things. Colin relaxed and Kate felt free to worry about the casserole again. Unnecessarily as it turned out, since she was so slow in producing the soup that the casserole had time to cook. And anyway, as Colin remarked later to Betty, they were so hungry by then that they would have eaten it half raw.

At first they had hardly recognised each other. When she came in from the kitchen, Kate had hesitated in the doorway, wondering who she was, this tall, elegant, beautifully coiffed woman, looking decorative in her sitting room. Then Betty had looked at her and smiled, that twisted little smile that she remembered on the face of the skinny, rebellious friend of her childhood, with the green eyes and long untidy fair hair that adults were always trying to tie in bunches or twist into plaits.

Betty, of course, had the advantage. She knew this must be Kate who came in from the kitchen wearing a pinafore and looking harassed. She was flushed but it suited her. The curly dark hair had obviously only been given the briefest of contact with a comb and make-up had consisted of a swift application of lipstick.

Their eyes met, they looked at each other with dawning recognition; it was as if the mask of adulthood slipped away and they saw each other again as children, like conspirators sharing a past. By the time they were half way through dinner, they were telling each other that they hadn't changed at all, not really.

'Do you go back to Netherby still, Kate?' Chrissie asked.

'Not very often now we've moved south. Only in my mind. I remember your father so well. He was a wonderful weather prophet. I can see him still, standing in the farm doorway looking up at the hills, reading the sky.'

Chrissie smiled.

'Fancy you remembering that,' she said.

'Oh, Kate always noticed things,' Betty put in. 'She was always getting into trouble for staring. It was the budding writer in her. All writers stare and listen. It's very unnerving.'

'And you? Did you get into trouble for anything?'

'Oh, I was always in trouble for everything.'

'Do you remember when Bisto killed the hen?'

'And when we slept under the stars?'

'Tell them about the cocoa,' Luke put in. 'You won't believe this, Jack, but they thought they'd be able to boil milk on a plant pot over a candle.'

'Well, we were only about ten,' Betty reminded him.

The women reminisced, the men listened, Colin finding it hard to picture his elegant wife as a tomboy, grateful that she had metamorphosed into a suitable partner for a prospective Member of Parliament.

'It's odd to think that all of us, four women, were brought up in Netherby,' Chrissie remarked, in a lull in the reminiscing. 'A pair of cousins and a pair of friends.'

'We stood on the village green and watched you drive to your wedding,' Betty said. 'I wonder if you noticed us?'

Chrissie laughed. 'I remember children standing by the roadside,' she said. 'Do you remember them, Nell?'

'No, I was too scared. The responsibility of being a brides-maid weighed heavily. I'd already forgotten your flowers, if you remember.'

'We were the scruffy pair,' Betty explained. 'And probably had my dog on a piece of string.'

'Betty told me you were a princess, Chrissie. And I believed her,' Kate said.

'She was always rather gullible,' Betty told them. 'Much more trusting than I was. You know, at Christmas we didn't give each other presents but just chose a book from the other one's shelf. But I always used to hide the ones I didn't want her to have, before I let her into my bedroom to choose.'

'I never realised! I know I was always terrified you'd choose one of my favourites. I used to put the Arthur Ransomes in the front because I never liked them. I couldn't see the point of all those kids' outings in boats. Maybe it had something to do with being brought up in the hills. I never took to watery adventures.'

'And I was scared you'd take one of my William books, so I always hid them.'

'I can't think why I didn't realise—'

'Oh, you weren't as worldly-wise as I was. And you did have a lot of books, Kate. Your father was always buying them for you.'

'It's all right. I'll forgive you.'

'Shall we add childhood memories to the banned list?' Colin suggested.

'Oh, I enjoy hearing them,' Luke said, getting up to open a window. 'It's a bit stuffy in here, isn't it?'

The evening was sultry.

'Shall we take the puddings outside?' Kate suggested, glancing round the table at her guests. She could see that by now they were all relaxed; the wine must be coursing through their veins, the casserole making them feel benevolent, all those little baby carrots and fresh spinach doing them a power of good. Stuffed full of vitamins they must be. Whatever the reason, their response was immediate and enthusiastic. They carried out bowls and plates and spoons and jugs of cream and arranged themselves round the big table on the top lawn. The air was soft against the skin; it reminded Kate of tropical evenings, but here it was still twilight.

They fell silent after the coffee, watching the darkness gather in the garden. Kate listened only abstractedly, her duty as hostess done. They were talking quietly, Jack and Luke about work, Nell and Colin, now all amiability, discussing something about current affairs, Betty and Chrissie putting in the odd remark, but really, like Kate, relishing the peace of the evening.

Earlier in the day, she had seen her garden awaken, opening up to the morning, and now she watched as it gathered itself together, closing in for the night. Slowly the light was fading, extinguishing the flowers one by one, first the blue and purple, then the pink and red and orange, until only the cream and white remained, gleaming in the twilight. The sweet smell of honeysuckle drifted up from the archway, mingling with the heavy scent of the philadelphus at the far corner of the garden, the white stars of its flowers still visible even as the first stars appeared in the sky.

Somebody yawned and said they must be going, but nobody stirred. Somebody else remarked that it had been a lovely evening, a delicious meal, but still they sat on. They are all subdued by the magic of the night, Kate thought, drugged by the sweet smells of it. The sky was full of stars now and even the white roses and lilies no longer glowed, translucent in the darkness. There was a dampness in the air as the dew began to fall: the peacefulness of the evening was tinged now with sadness. She had quite forgotten, she suddenly realised, to say anything about her novel. Strange that something that had been so important in her life for the past two years should seem, on such an evening, quite insignificant.

Chapter Six

'So she was right,' Betty said, turning off the radio.

'Who?'

'Nell, of course. Don't you remember? When you kept saying the Prime Minister wouldn't put up VAT? She's damned near doubled it.'

Colin shrugged.

'We have to be realistic,' he said. 'If she'd said she was going to double VAT she wouldn't have got elected.'

'So lying doesn't matter any more?'

'Let's just say that it is sometimes necessary for a politician to be economical with the truth.'

'And you? Would you be "economical with the truth" to get elected?'

'What's your guess? I'd take my cue from my leader, wouldn't I?'

She didn't reply. Part of her was appalled by him. But a sneaky little part was impressed by the calculating cynicism of this man she had married, as if she had discovered hidden depths in him, an unexpected thrill. All the same, she couldn't help wondering what Nell was thinking.

'Hankerton's not standing next time,' Colin was saying. 'I might be in with a chance there. Though being a pretty safe seat, I don't expect they'd offer it to a new boy like me.'

Instead a rather more marginal seat came his way two years later. The Labour MP had got in at Boxley with a much reduced majority. The Tory candidate, disenchanted with his government, had announced his intention of not standing at the next election. Colin's name was on the selection list.

'The first step on the ladder,' he said, opening the champagne. 'You'll come with me, of course?'

'Of course.'

'I don't know what the form is. Well, I know I talk for about half an hour and then answer questions.'

'Don't worry, we'll suss it all out in good time.'

Now that it was actually happening, she was beginning to feel the excitement of it. 'And I'll be with you all the way,' she added enthusiastically.

They raised their glasses and drank to his future, Colin remembering just in time not to say 'Cheers', because someone had told him that it was vulgar.

'And if you do me the honour of choosing me for your candidate,' Colin ended his speech, 'I shall, of course, immediately come and live in the constituency.'

Betty heard his words with some surprise; it was the first she'd heard of it. They'd talked about what they would do if he was elected. As an MP he'd certainly buy a house in Boxley, but that was a long way off. This business of the candidacy was imminent.

'Got carried away, did you?' she asked him afterwards.

'No. I thought you'd realised we'd have to move.'

Defensive, as always, when he'd misled.

'It's all right,' she told him. 'I wouldn't mind giving up my career for a while to have babies.'

'Oh, yes, that.'

Colin was divided in his mind about this business of having a family. On the one hand there would be votes in being a family man. On the other he certainly didn't want her pregnant at election time. He needed her to be in good shape then; she'd be invaluable canvassing for him and sitting elegantly with him on platforms.

'We'll think about it later,' he hedged. 'I'm not even a candidate yet and might never be.'

But he was. In February 1982 he was adopted as their candidate by the Boxley constituency in Surrey.

'Includes a bit of the Stockbroker Belt,' he told Betty. 'Would have been ideal for me in more auspicious times.'

But the times were not auspicious.

'Just my luck to be standing now,' he grumbled, 'when that bloody woman's made such a cock-up of everything.'

Unemployment, broken tax promises, cuts in education, the collapse of manufacturing industry, these and much else had sent the government's popularity spiralling downwards. At the procession to the royal wedding, the Prime Minister had been booed.

'We'll be routed at the next election,' Colin foretold.

But the Falklands changed all that. And in the following years he played that card for all it was worth. Sometimes it wasn't worth much. At one meeting in the constituency he declaimed, 'The Prime Minister may have done some harsh things and even made a few mistakes in her first two years, but without her we wouldn't have won the Falklands War.'

'Without her we wouldn't have had a Falklands War,' shouted one of the audience.

There had been a lot of clapping.

'Maybe you shouldn't use that line quite so much now,' Betty suggested.

She was not very optimistic about his chances. She knew how dismayed he would be by defeat.

'Don't worry,' Colin said. 'I have it on good authority that there are going to be plenty of tax sweeteners before the next election. Tax cuts are real vote winners.'

'But Nell was telling me that we actually pay more in taxation than we did before. Tax hasn't been cut, just moved sideways and increased in the process. That's what Nell says.'

'She would.'

'Is it true?'

'Well, yes. But the point is, Betty, that people don't notice when they're paying VAT. They just think that the price has gone up. They soon forget that it's a tax at all. But they *do* notice income tax. That's why we're moving taxes from direct to indirect.'

'Oh, come off it, Colin. People aren't as stupid as that.'

'Oh, yes they are. They're every bit as stupid as that. Shall I tell you the advice I was given by a chap at central office? He said, "Never underestimate the stupidity of the electorate. You can fool them again and again. With the same trick."'

'But that's awful.'

'No, it's not. It's realistic.'

Increasingly, she had observed, he confused realism with cynicism.

'But, Colin, what's the point of being an MP if you don't really believe in the people you represent?'

'But I do believe in them. At least I believe that it's good

59

for them that I, and like-minded people, should have power.'

'That's what it's all about, isn't it? Power?'

He nodded. 'Of course,' he said.

She enjoyed the campaigning much more than she'd expected to. It was a challenge and the people were fun to work with. It made such a change from her usual work. She entered into it wholeheartedly. Colin could charm people; she watched him with increasing respect. He was physically strong too; she hadn't realised before how tough MPs need to be. Even he, by the end of the campaign, looked tired and had almost lost his voice. He was going to be shattered if he lost now. She couldn't care less about politics but she desperately wanted him to win.

And win he did; he turned a Labour majority of four thousand into a majority for himself of over a thousand and they were up most of the night celebrating. When they fell into bed at five in the morning, she expected to sleep and was astonished that he wanted to spend their only two hours' rest in passionate love-making. So it was true, she thought; power is the great aphrodisiac.

Chapter Seven

For a while, the reality of being a Member of Parliament subdued Colin. He hadn't expected to feel so nervous, so overawed by it all. He felt like a new boy as he stood in Members' Lobby. He was terrified of doing the wrong thing at rituals like electing the Speaker, or of sitting in the wrong place in the Members' dining room. All his old social insecurity flooded back; he might have been eighteen again, embarrassed by his parents when they came to visit him at Cambridge, his father loudly proclaiming that there'd been nothing like this in their day, while his mother kept on about his meals and laundry.

He had made sure that they wouldn't come again, inventing lectures, seminars, tutorials, anything to keep them away. They didn't understand the system, so it wasn't difficult to manoeuvre them out of his life. All the same, a great weight seemed to have been lifted from him when his parents died. He felt free of his past, free to be what he now considered to be himself. It went far to alleviate his grief.

He was immensely pleased that Betty had never known them. She wasn't a snob, but it would have been bound to affect her view of him. Anyway he was relieved that in their considerate and unassuming way they had effaced themselves, with cancer, before she appeared on the scene.

He was grateful too that nowadays the fact of not having been to a public school would not impede his career. He managed to imply to his new friends that for ideological reasons his parents had sent him to state schools, suggesting that his father was something of a character, an eccentric really, a bit left-wing in his idiosyncratic way. It was a pity they would never meet him, he would say, for they would have found him very amusing, very droll.

Having reinvented bits of his life and eradicated others, he began expressing opinions to befit his new persona, proclaiming himself 'A True Blue', in the hope that the shade of his politics might somehow colour his blood.

He had been surprised when his friends took him up on this; why not stand for Parliament? they'd asked him. Such a thing had never entered his head at first; he didn't come from a class that did such things, had been his initial reaction. Then he realised that he did now, of course he did. He had created himself as a person who came from a family that might well have stood for Parliament. Thus he had begun the journey that ended with him standing nervously in Members' Lobby, feeling like a new boy.

He was not a man to feel nervous for long. His unremarkable maiden speech successfully delivered, he soon settled comfortably into the House, aware of being probably one of the richest and certainly the best-looking of the new intake of MPs of any party.

'What we need to do now,' he told Betty, over a late breakfast one Sunday morning, 'is to establish ourselves more firmly in the constituency, make our presence felt here, become a really central part of the social scene. For a start—'

'Seven letters beginning with L,' she said, looking up from the crossword.

'Betty, I—'

'And the clue's extraordinary. It just says NIAP.'

'There's no such word,' he said impatiently, distracted for a moment from his theme.

'I've checked to make sure. Just in case it was a Scottish archaicism or the former currency of some now uninhabited island or some other obscure thing I've never heard of. But there's nothing in the dictionary, nothing at all.'

She looked at the paper.

'It's got G for the next to last letter,' she said. 'If that's any help.'

'Betty, can't you just leave it for a while?'

'But I've nearly finished, Colin. It's the last one. Oh, I've had a thought. Could NIAP be the initials of a quango?'

'If so, I've never heard of it.'

'They're sprouting up all over the place, these quangos, aren't they? I must say I'd never heard of them until the last election, when we were told they were all going to be abolished. The only difference seems to be they're paid a lot now and they used to be voluntary.'

'Maybe, but that's not what we're discussing at the moment. As I was saying, we need to share more in the social scene. For a start we need a bigger house and—'

Startled, she put down the newspaper.

'But this one's quite big enough, Colin,' she objected.

'It's not just a matter of size. I mean we ought to have something more in keeping with our position, a family seat as it were, you know the sort of thing.'

Ah, a family home; if that was what he meant, she certainly wanted it. When she had given up her job to go and live in the Boxley constituency and start a family, she had thought she was making a great sacrifice. No more big salary, no more generous allowances, no more exotic travel; it was a lot to give up, she'd thought, just so she could have a baby.

But she didn't. The thing didn't happen. Soon she realised that the deprivation of a career was as nothing compared with the deprivation of childlessness. You knew you could always go back to a career, or make a new one. But you couldn't know about having a baby. You might never have one. The thought of it, the emptiness of it, appalled her. Each month she hoped – and each month she despaired.

Colin told her not to worry; give it time, he said.

Frankly, although he was too tactful to say so, he didn't much mind either way. Certainly, being a family man could be an electoral asset. Children provided something for constituents to enquire about and they looked good on election pamphlets. Prime Ministers liked the sound of a family man too. After the next election he should be in line for promotion. 'A hard-working, reliable chap,' he could imagine the Chief Whip advising. 'Good family man, too, Prime Minister.'

But there was a lot to be said for not having children; childless couples are free to entertain and to be entertained, no complications about nannies or childish ailments which he'd seen wreak such havoc in the households of colleagues. It would be good to know that he could always be sure of having Betty there, free to move between London and Boxley, healthy, energetic and elegant.

So he came down on the side of not worrying. But she did worry; all the time, the anxiety was there.

'Shall I make you an appointment, so you can go for tests?' she asked, in what seemed to him a sudden change of topic when he'd been talking about having a grander house.

'Oh, honestly, darling! Take a look at my diary. I've something every day. Can't we leave it for a while? At least till the recess?'

'You don't like the idea of tests, do you?' she hazarded.

'What man does? Checking up on your virility!'

'Fertility is not the same as virility, idiot,' she told him.

'Not medically, maybe. Anyway what's the hurry?'

'I want to start doing something about it, before it's too late.'

'Look, Betty, you mustn't get obsessive about this thing. There's plenty you can do to keep your mind off it.'

'I know that. I'm always busy here. I'm a sitting duck for anyone who wants a hand with every fête and jumble sale, but that's not the point. I gave up work expressly to settle in the constituency and start a family. I've done that for you, Colin. It's time you played your part.'

'But I do play my part,' he mocked, coming round to her side of the table and beginning to caress her. 'Regularly. And I'm standing by now, actually. At your service all morning.'

She removed his hands, determined not to be distracted.

'I mean it, Colin,' she said firmly. 'I do want to make a start now. Promise me you'll fix that appointment.'

He hesitated. He looked at her; the green eyes looked straight back at him, her hands wrapped the negligee firmly around her, shutting him out. Then she turned back to the crossword.

'I get the message,' he said. 'I'll make an appointment as soon as I can find the time.'

'You don't *find* time, Colin, you have to *make* it.'

'I've promised, haven't I? Now why don't we go back to bed?'

'Lumbago,' she said.

'*What?* You've got *lumbago?*'

'Yes. It's the answer. NIAP spells back pain. So the answer's lumbago. Quite neat really.'

'My God, what twisted minds these crossword composers must have,' he said.

Then he leant over her again, his hands caressing, and this time she didn't stop him.

Chapter Eight

'But it's a mansion,' Betty protested, when Colin parked the car with a flourish in front of the Georgian manor he had told her he wanted to buy.

They had driven what seemed like half a mile up a drive bordered with rhododendron bushes through which she had glimpsed lawns and a lake with trees beyond. Then suddenly they had swung into a great circle in front of the house, where, with much splattering of gravel, they had stopped in front of impressive steps, curved and balustraded, leading up to a wide front door topped with a shell-shaped canopy.

'And I have the key to that door,' Colin said, speaking slowly, as if the words had metaphorical significance.

'But it's enormous. I'd no idea it was anything like this.'

'I thought I'd surprise you.'

'You have.'

'Come on.'

He took her arm and led her up the steps, took the key, with the estate agent's label, and opened the door.

It was a welcoming house. It didn't strike cold and damp the way most empty buildings do. It faced due south; when they opened the door the midday sun streamed across the great stone-flagged hall, brightening the graceful curved staircase at the back.

'I feel like a trespasser,' she said.

'Nonsense. And why are you speaking in whispers?'

'Because I feel as if I'm in a National Trust property and their guides make me nervous. Any moment now someone will ask to see my ticket. However many rooms does it have?'

'Nine bedrooms, not counting box rooms. I think some could be converted into bathrooms. There are four big reception rooms. Come and look.'

The drawing room shutters were closed. She stood in the dim

light while Colin folded them back. A view across the lawns to the lake and the rolling countryside beyond was suddenly revealed, as if a picture had been held up at the window.

'Like it?' he asked.

'Oh, Colin, it is so beautiful. I love it. But we couldn't possibly afford it.'

'No reason why not. Come and see the rest.'

He paused at the foot of the stairs, looking up.

'Impressive, isn't it?' he said.

He stood for a moment imagining the rich and great of the past ascending and descending those stairs. He pictured the grandeur of them. He felt a frisson of excitement, of triumph as he remembered the semi-detached villa of his youth. He had arrived. He had made it. His parents would only have seen the inside of a house like this as tourists, or, in earlier times, as servants. He allowed himself a moment of exultation, then he put his youth, his childhood home and his parents back into the limbo where they belonged. He took his elegant wife by the hand and led her upstairs.

'This would be our bedroom, above the drawing room,' he said, opening the shutters to reveal the same view of the lake as they had seen from the drawing room. Only from up here it was a wider, longer vista; the whole countryside seemed to unfold below them. She stood at the window, gazing out.

'There's a dressing room which we could convert into an en suite bathroom,' he was saying.

She decided to indulge him, share in his fantasy. It was no good trying to talk sensibly while they were here. Afterwards, away from the magic of the place, she would make him see sense.

'It might be better, actually, to leave it as a dressing room,' she said, 'and convert that little bedroom next door into a bathroom. You could easily make a doorway through to it.'

He agreed instantly and they walked from room to room, converting, altering, modernising, improving. It was a lovely game, she thought.

'I wish I'd brought sandwiches,' she said, as they locked the front door behind them. 'We could have had a picnic by the lake, under that weeping willow.'

'I'm glad you didn't. We'll go and find a decent lunch somewhere. Not in the village, I think. We don't want to start rumours. I think there's a place called the Old Mill Restaurant not too far away. I've got the *Good Food Guide* in the car; we'll look it up.'

The table was outside, under an awning, by the mill stream, very quiet and private. Here they could talk.

'Look, darling,' she began. 'It's a lovely house, but way beyond us. I mean I haven't even dared ask you how much.'

She gasped when he told her. Then laughed.

'It's all just been a tease, hasn't it?'

'I'm serious, Betty. We're settled in the constituency now. We might be here for the rest of our lives. We need the right sort of house, where we can entertain. This suits our image. You should see the kind of houses *some* of my colleagues live in. They're far grander than this.'

'Oh, Colin, that does sound a bit like keeping up with the Joneses. There's nothing wrong with the house we've got. And wasn't it a wise man who said, "Never try to keep up with the Joneses. Drag them down to your own level. It's cheaper"?'

He gave her a hard look. All right for her to joke about it. She'd been brought up in a big house in the country, hadn't she?

'A house like this,' he said, 'is a good investment. Property values have increased astronomically in recent years. It can't be wrong to put your money into bricks and mortar.'

'They don't always increase. There have been slumps in the housing market. It could happen again. People have been saddled with big houses they couldn't sell.'

'Not now they won't. Think how enormous the rates are on houses like this.'

'Exactly. I have thought.'

'But the PM is going to change all that, Betty. It's common knowledge at Westminster. I'm in the know about such things now, and I tell you the Poll Tax is a winner and she's determined to get it through as soon as possible. And they're all supporting her – Baker, Ridley, Fowler, everyone who matters. The flagship of the Tory party, they're going to call it.'

'But how does that affect us?'

'When the Poll Tax comes in, the owner of this house will pay the same as the chap who lives in a one-up-one-down in some back street in Birmingham.'

'So?'

'So the big houses will keep their value, even if the others fall.'

'All right. But the upkeep on that place will be horrific.'

'We can afford it. By the way, all your overseas shares are doing well.'

She had handed over to him the management of all her capital.

'Why overseas? Why don't you invest in Great Britain PLC?'

'I wouldn't invest my clients' money in a *company* that sold its assets and used the proceeds on current account, so I don't invest in a *country* that's doing that either.'

'So you take one view as a politician and another as a financier?'

'Of course. I do know about money, Betty. And I can tell you we live in good times for anyone in the City.'

'Not boom and bust?'

He looked quite shocked. 'Really! Betty! Mind you, I don't take risks. I hedge my assets. For example, the house will be in your name, so that if anything did go wrong it would still be ours. Everyone takes measures to ensure that their assets are safe from the receiver. It's only common sense. You do trust me, don't you?'

She leant across the table and took his hands. Of course she trusted him. More than ever. And loved him more than ever. Politics suited him. Since entering the House, he had grown in confidence, he even looked bigger, more assertive, better groomed, more poised. The slight greying at the temples gave him a distinguished look. People in the know were saying that he was a man to watch, a man with a future. Besides, the way that the women in the party played up to him, flattering him, made her more aware of his charms. Made him seem somehow of more value, more worth cherishing. Put in economic terms, he had a certain scarcity value and the demand for him was increasing. Therefore his price went up in her eyes.

'And there's another thing,' he was saying. 'It's been suggested to me that I might become a Name.'

'A Lloyds Name? You mean a member?'

'What else?'

'Isn't it risky?'

He shook his head.

'Money for jam,' he said. 'A guaranteed twenty-five grand a year for doing nothing.'

'Nothing is for nothing. What about the risk?'

'There hasn't been a claim for as long as anyone can remember.'

Chapter Nine

'Shall I get you the forms for delivering the post this Christmas?'
Chrissie asked, glancing up from stirring Christmas puddings,
which she always made in September, as her daughter came into
the kitchen.

'Oh, don't bother, Mum. I'm not going to do it this year.'

'Oh, why not? I thought you always enjoyed it. You'll still be
needing the extra money, won't you?'

'This chap Ray, on my course, says his father's advised him to
buy telephone shares and sell them a bit later. So in November
I'm going to invest my allowance for next term, plus a bit I've
got in the building society, in these shares, then sell them when
he tells me to. He says that I'd make more money doing that than
working for two weeks delivering the mail.'

'But it's useful, doing the post. And it taught you that letters
don't just arrive on the mat. Somebody has to struggle through
the wind and rain to deliver them.'

'Come off it, Mum. Why work when you can get more money
for doing nothing? He said it would only take half an hour
to fill up the forms and it's a guaranteed profit. Money for
jam.'

Chrissie didn't reply. It was the voice of the Eighties and there
was no arguing with it.

In bed that night she said to Jack, 'I sometimes think we've brought
them up all wrong.'

'Nonsense, they're fine.'

'But we've brought them up to care about people the way it
used to be. Now they're surrounded on all sides by voices telling
them there's nothing wrong with being greedy—'

'There's a lot wrong with being greedy,' Jack cut in. 'You and
I know that.'

'But,' Chrissie persisted, 'what are they to make of it? It must be confusing for Claire—'

He smiled. 'Claire's always been a bit confused,' he told her. 'But she's all right, just taking her time about growing up.'

Chrissie smiled. 'Yes, you're right. She's still a mixture. For all she can be so hard, she does take things to heart and she's wonderful with Rosemary. Mrs Rawley says she's like a second mother to her.'

'She's turning into a stunner too.'

'Oh, do you think so? I suppose I never think of the girls like that. I'm too close to them. Certainly she's not like either of us, is she?'

'That's true.'

There was no doubt whose daughter Sarah was, Jack thought. She was well-built like her mother, she had the same open face and golden hair. She looked a country girl, wholesome and beautiful. But Claire, wherever did her looks come from?

'I wish I'd known your parents,' Chrissie said, her thoughts in tandem.

'She's a bit like my mother, I suppose.'

She waited for him to go on, but he said no more. He could still see his mother as she lay in bed, her dark hair spread across the pillow, so soon after his father died. Peaceful in death, she was, sleeping the sleep of one who has got the overdose just right.

There had been a tension about his mother, highly-strung they used to call her. But she was a very good-looking woman in a gypsy-like kind of way. Claire had that same tension; there was something electric about her, a magnetic attraction. A fair-haired gypsy, was his younger daughter. She did not have the serene beauty of her mother and sister. Her looks were of a different quality, arresting, faintly alarming.

'She doesn't seem to have the number of boyfriends that Sarah does,' her mother said.

'Maybe she frightens them? She's probably a bit of a challenge, you know, Chrissie, to a young man. They're much less confident, these young chaps, than they make out. I can imagine her going for an older man.'

'I don't like the sound of that,' Chrissie said, frowning.

Jack ran his fingers gently across her brow.

'Don't worry about her, Chrissie. Think how you used to worry about Sarah and she's turned out fine.'

She smiled up at him. 'But I do still worry about her too. She's a selfless girl and that's how we'd want her to be, but I sometimes wonder if that really fits her to get on in a world where greed is somehow right, almost a virtue?'

'There's always been greed,' he told her, but he knew what she meant all the same. Now it had become official, smiled upon, sanctified.

He drew her close, kissed her gently.

'It needn't affect us,' he said. 'If the politicians want to preach greed, let them. We keep to our own way of thinking.'

'But, Jack, we can't.'

She shook her head, puzzled by his naivety. 'It's all round them, the atmosphere has changed. They're bound to be affected. I see it in hospital.'

'How?'

'Oh, a kind of callousness. All the management seem to care about is making the statistics look good so the politicians can say we're treating more patients than ever before.'

'Incidentally, has there ever been a time when we didn't treat more patients than ever before?'

Chrissie laughed. 'No, of course not. There have always been more, each year.'

She sighed. 'I'm sorry, Jack. How has your day been?'

'Grim. We're having to cut back on all the apprenticeship schemes. There just isn't the work to support the cost.'

'But I thought you used to say that all the oil money would be spent on houses and transport and waterworks and all those things. You were so hopeful.'

'I'm sorry, Chrissie.'

He spoke without irony. It had always been his role to keep her well-informed on such matters and he had misled her. He put his hands behind his head, propped up against the pillows, beginning one of his lectures, Chrissie realised.

'You see a country is like any other property, Chrissie,' he began. 'You have to keep it in good repair. If you neglect it, like a bad housekeeper, it will only cost you much more in the long run.'

She thought of the farm where she had been brought up, her father always mending and repairing all the farm buildings. He would have agreed with what Jack was saying. He'd no use for farmers who neglected their buildings, their gates and their dry-stone walls.

'We're training a whole generation of young people to depend on the state for hand-outs. Young chaps who in the past we'd have been training on sites all over the country. If they'd been working hard on site all day they wouldn't have the energy to get up to mischief. And they'd be with older men. They need that. Not always to be hanging about with their own age group. They need to be occupied. All parents know that.'

'Claire says a lot of her friends are on the dole.'

'Has she said any more about what she wants to do?'

'Not teach. She's dropped that altogether. It seems a pity after she did the teacher training course but she said that when she went round schools they were all demoralised.'

'So?'

'She thinks perhaps something to do with computers. She could do it after the secretarial course she's on now. And she says the pay would be better.'

'Well, there's no harm in having secretarial qualifications as well as a degree, Chrissie.'

'No, I suppose not. But I've always thought she'd be good at teaching. She's lively, she'd keep the children on their toes. But . . .'

She hesitated. Loyalty to her children made criticism difficult, even to Jack.

'Go on.'

'She seems harder somehow. As if all these attitudes have rubbed off on her. She used to enjoy delivering the Christmas mail, she liked doing that kind of thing for people. Young people always like to help. But now nothing seems to be valued unless there's money in it. Easy money too.'

'It's the way of the world just now, I'm afraid, Chrissie.'

'I suppose so,' she said resignedly. 'But it's awful somehow to see it happening to your own family.'

Chapter Ten

'And we'll ask anybody who is anybody to the housewarming,' Colin said largely.

Betty laughed. 'If you could see the place now you wouldn't even dare to think the words,' she told him.

'I shan't see it for a couple of weeks now. But I'm sure the men have got everything under control,' he told her confidently, as he gave her a quick peck on the cheek. 'Must be off now. London calls. Join me tomorrow?'

'I don't think I can. There's so much to do at this end.'

'Well, not later than Wednesday. I'll ring you tonight after the vote.'

It was ten o'clock before she got to the manor house. The men were having their break. She had lost count of how many they were employing. There must be about twenty-five of them ranged round the big drawing room, leaning back against the walls, sandwich boxes on knees, thermos flasks alongside, copies of the *Sun*, *Express* and *Mail* widespread. There was a smell of strong tea and potato crisps.

The men had chosen that room as their base. It was big enough to store what looked like hundreds of tins of paint and rolls of wallpaper, carpets which had been delivered far too soon, unlike most things which arrived far too late, three baths, eight basins and four lavatories. A double sink unit leant against the fireplace and the bookshelves were stacked with boxes of taps. Four candelabras squatted awkwardly in a corner, awaiting the attention of the electrician. She had wanted to store some of this stuff in the outhouses with all the other materials but the carpenter, who seemed to act as foreman, said it was too precious, might get damaged. So the drawing room was a cross between a warehouse and a wayside cafe. She was glad they had decided to carpet it; at least she needn't worry about the rings left on the parquet floor by mugs of tea, or the burn marks of cigarette stubs.

'The decorator would like a word,' the carpenter said to her now.

'Oh, yes, you're going to get on with the main bedroom and bathroom today, aren't you?'

The decorator shook his head.

'We're waiting on the carpenter,' he said. 'Can't start until he's boxed in them pipes.'

'Can he do that today?'

'Bert, can you box in that pipework in the bathroom today?'

'No. Timber hasn't arrived. Carters promised it for Friday but it didn't come.'

'Shall I ring?' she volunteered.

'Telephone's off again. The engineer won't be back till tomorrow.'

'I thought the telephones were to be all ready by the end of last week?'

'Ran out of cable. And they can't complete on the burglar alarm until their own electrician makes the link-up. Telephone engineers aren't allowed to do that.'

'And anyway,' the carpenter said, 'Mike wants me to finish working in the study. The plumber can't fix the radiator until I've altered the wainscot.'

'Oh, and the mason asked me to say that he's repointed the chimney at the back but he's not at all happy about the roof round there. The slates are slipping. Some of 'em cracked. He reckons they got damaged, way back, by men fixing the television aerial. They dance around on them slates without showing proper respect. Not even the right shoes on their feet often as not, he says. You could have a leak there if we had heavy rain.'

'I'll have a word with him—'

'He's not here. He's gone off to another job. He might be back here Wednesday afternoon. It depends how they get on.'

'But we can't risk rain coming in. That's over the little upstairs study that we're decorating now. We don't want rainwater damaging the only room we've finished.'

The carpenter shook his head.

'It's not finished,' he said. 'The decorator couldn't start because the electrician hadn't changed the light switch.'

'The light switch?'

'You remember your husband wanted the door opening the other way to make room for a bookcase? The carpenter's rehung the door, but now the light switch's on the wrong side. So the electrician'll have to rewire it.'

'Can he do that now?'

'Not till the plumber's swung down the radiator. And he's fixing the kitchen today. Priority he said it was.'

'I'll have a word with him about it.'

The men were getting up now, packing away sandwich boxes, replacing caps on thermos flasks, folding newspapers. The unnatural silence of the lunchbreak, Betty knew, was over. As the men dispersed about the house, transistor radios were switched on, electric drills started to whine, hammering began anew. She could hear the carpenter, who had a powerful pair of lungs, launch into his repertoire of songs of two world wars. His mate didn't sing, but had a penetrating whistle. Pete, the decorator's boy, always known as ''Enery', broke into his endless recitative of "Enery the Heighth I am, I am, 'Enery the Heighth I am,' repeating the same words over and over again, knowing no others.

She saw the plumber, who was easy to distinguish from the other men because he always wore a red woollen hat, walk over to the fireplace and pick up the double sink unit. He was a powerful little man with a stooping walk, swift and ape-like, as if he had adapted his way of moving to cramped spaces around pipes, under floors and in attics.

She followed him into the kitchen, hardly able to keep up with him, although he was encumbered with pressed steel.

He looked at her gloomily.

'Short of a gate lock and a crutch-handled stopcock,' he said, staring accusingly down at a pile of plumbing materials. 'And if you want the sink raised, it'll need a telescopic P trap.'

'Would they send them?'

He shook his head.

'No. I have to go and queue for them at the plumbers' merchants in Didsbury.'

'If I went to get them for you, could you get on with something else? Oh, the electrician would like you to swing down the radiator in the study.'

'That's a two-minute job.'

'And the outside tap. Perhaps you could install the outside tap?'

'I could – if I had an angled bib tap and another compression elbow.'

'I'll get them. So, is there anything else you could do while you're waiting?'

'Depends how long you are. I've all the piping and junctions to do yet.'

'How long will that take?'

'About a week.'

She laughed.

'Well, where is this place? Could you draw me a map?'

He took a pencil out of his hat and, squatting down beside her, drew a map on the floorboards.

She watched him, then, 'So do I take the floor with me?' she asked.

He grinned up at her. He liked her. She was a one, she was.

'Make sure there's threaded nozzle on the bib tap,' he said. 'And tell them it's a fifteen millimetre wall-plate elbow you want. They may call it a bib tap flange, but it makes no odds. But make sure it's a threaded nozzle they give you.'

She found paper, brought in a road map from the car. She wrote down exactly what he wanted. Then she went round all the other rooms listing what was being done, what materials were needed and went off with a shopping list to join the queue of tradesmen, first at the plumbers' suppliers and then at the builders'. Tonight she would tell Colin she couldn't possibly come to London. She had to be here to organise things; otherwise this house would never be ready to live in, let alone receive guests at a housewarming party.

The carpenter watched her drive off.

'She'd have made a grand foreman, she would,' he told the plumber. 'Pity she's only a woman.'

Chapter Eleven

What she really ought to do, Claire decided at the beginning of the summer holidays, was to sit back and look at her problems, most particularly what she was going to do with her life. She had always felt it must be something momentous; she caught glimpses of what it might be, but could never quite pin it down.

There had been a time when she had thought she had a religious vocation. Hoping for divine revelation, the reality of what life in a religious order actually involved had proved, on further investigation, a bitter disappointment.

Grand passion replaced the religious calling; nobody, she felt sure, with the possible exception of Emma Bovary, had ever loved so ardently. The object of her passion was the geography tutor whom she worshipped from afar. Her love was total and it was selfless. When her worshipping grew less distant, she found that he was kind, gentle and homosexual.

She had felt inspired by this unhappy experience to write a novel. The vague ideas that floated about in her mind were recognisably the stuff of great literature, immensely moving whether tragic or comic, but when she tried to put them into words, there was no greatness, indeed there was nothing at all. In short she couldn't think what to put. It was maddening really considering she had all these marvellous ideas; it was just the words that let her down.

She tried talking to Sarah about it, but she only suggested that Claire was mistaking for grander emotions and talents what were really just the yearnings of her delayed adolescence. Which was nonsense and the sort of thing an elder sister would say. She had consulted her mother's friend Kate, who wrote books, but she'd just said something about Trusting to your Subconscious, which had been no help at all.

The trouble was that most jobs seemed such a terrible waste of one's youth. It amazed her that other people didn't seem to feel this; maybe it was because she was destined for something special. There was Sarah, for example, actually enjoying teaching, or so she made out, when really she was just letting her youth slip by. She was using up her twenties, Sarah was, and what would she have to show for it? She, Claire, was determined that she would have something to show for it, something great and remarkable. It was just that she couldn't decide what. She sometimes thought that she might go in for being an entrepreneur.

'I'm sorry I wasn't able to help Claire more,' Kate said to Chrissie on the phone. 'She rang me, you know, about a career in writing.'

'Oh, she has lots of ideas like that—'

'It's so difficult to help and people always seem to think that just because I've had three books published, I'll be able to help them. But it isn't like that, I'm afraid. Still I did wonder afterwards if I might perhaps have—'

'Please don't worry about it,' Chrissie interrupted. 'I'm sure Claire's forgotten all about it now.'

'I can't even help *myself* just now, let alone anyone else,' Kate said, as she rang off.

She picked up the letter she had been reading, first with joy and then with increasing alarm, when Chrissie had rung. It was from her agent.

Dear Kate,

I read your novel with great pleasure. The characterisation is excellent, you pack in a great deal of interesting comment and the whole thing is spiced with humour.

May I take this opportunity of suggesting a few alterations which might make the book even better?

The central figure of the artist is very well drawn. You have succeeded in making us care about the man and to feel that he is a good, even great, artist. But he isn't very successful, is he?

It is hard nowadays to sell fiction in which the hero seems to be a loser. It occurred to me that you might perhaps make him a commercial artist; they are doing very well at present. He could design logos; there's a lot of money in logos. I was amazed at the amount we had to spend when we redesigned ours. I just feel that he needs more financial motivation.

My other anxiety is about your heroine. One is moved by her situation, the tragedy of the baby, her being so stricken by the treachery of her friend, but the modern woman doesn't want to identify with this sort of thing. Perhaps Emma could just be a bit tired and go on a cruise to somewhere exotic instead? She could perhaps meet a lover in some tropical island?

And then there is the ending. I do realise that with this new scenario you wouldn't be able to keep your final chapter in which she comes to terms with the past. It is very moving but it isn't very televisual, is it? And we do have to consider the subsidiary rights. Spin-off is very important. It really helps if you can bear this in mind when you are writing your novel.

So I think you may have to sacrifice the present ending, good though it is in its own way, and replace it with something more positive. Perhaps she could return to England with this lover who turns out to be a budding entrepreneur with whom she goes into partnership? Then she could realise her potential as a tough and successful business woman?

Also, I'm not too happy about the rather companionable marriage of the Hanningtons. I can see why you have made it like that, given their characters and background, but I feel you might make it a bit more tempestuous. A bit more meaty, if you see what I mean. Readers are accustomed to stronger stuff. Perhaps you could expand the passages I have marked with an asterisk and introduce a little more physicality?

When you have dealt with these suggestions, I should be delighted to see the script again. As I say, I think it is a splendid novel and with these rewrites could be your best yet.

With best wishes,

Veronica.

She made herself re-read it. Still she could make no sense of it. After a mug of coffee, it occurred to her that it might be a joke; it read like a parody. Better to laugh than to cry. But then the letters that she had had from this new appointee at Hindley's had often read like parodies. And hadn't been.

'Perhaps you should try,' Luke suggested that night, 'to meet her half way, compromise. I don't know if that's possible . . .' He spoke nervously; he was always conscious of walking on very thin ice in any discussion of Kate's writing. His own work involved concrete problems and solutions. He was well aware that Kate's work was made of more tenuous material. When she was miserable with her writing, he desperately wanted to help her, but didn't know how. The fact that probably nobody knew how, was small consolation.

She saw this and loved him for it.

'I'll have a go,' she said.

But it didn't work, could not work.

'I'd rather give it up and do something quite different,' she said. 'It would be more honest.'

He didn't know what to say. It wasn't something he understood. He stood helplessly by, knowing how much it mattered to her but not really understanding why.

'Why not ring her again,' he suggested. 'Try to find out what it's all about.'

'But I *know* what it's all about. It's all about pandering to a nineteen-eighties fashion, it's all about writing for a market that's supposed to want a diet of sex that's violent and violence that's kind of sexy and—'

'Perhaps,' Luke cut in, bravely for her sake playing devil's advocate, 'you have to accept that that is, in fact, what people *do* want.'

'But it's not true. I wouldn't mind so much if the agency were right about it, if that really was what everyone wanted to read. But they're not right. The readers say they're sick to death of this kind of stuff; they tell authors, they tell librarians but still it doesn't get through to the decision-makers.'

He looked at her helplessly.

'I really can't think what to suggest,' he said.

He looked so woebegone at his inability to help her that she couldn't bear it and said, 'Yes, you're right. I'll ring her and see what it's all about. Thank you. You're always such a support.'

He took her in his arms, happy that he'd been able to help, and she returned his embrace happy that he was happy, but also well aware that ringing Veronica wouldn't make the slightest difference and that she already knew what it was all about: it was all about not taking on her book unless she altered it.

'You see,' Veronica said, 'the people who make decisions about

80

your book are thirty-four, on their second divorce and living in Kensington.'

'But my readers aren't,' Kate objected. 'They're all sorts of different people.'

Even as she spoke she knew it sounded naive, knew she had lost the argument.

'Well, I'm sorry about it,' Veronica was saying, 'but you know we are all market-driven nowadays. If you do find you can write the sort of thing I can sell, you will get in touch, won't you? And of course if you can do those rewrites on this script I'd be delighted to see it again.'

'Thank you,' Kate said and rang off.

She put the manuscript away unaltered, then she went into the garden and did some vigorous weeding all morning. In the afternoon, determinedly domesticated, she made biscuits from a recipe which Chrissie had given her.

'Why can't we have proper *bought* biscuits like everyone else?' Daniel demanded at tea-time.

But then he ate so many that she had to hide the tin in the back of the cupboard in case there weren't any left for Betty who was coming over tomorrow for the day.

Chapter Twelve

'Colin's been made a PPS,' Betty told Kate, as they carried their coffee into the garden. Then, seeing her friend's baffled look, she added, 'It means Parliamentary Private Secretary.'

'Oh, and I always thought it was something at the end of a letter.'

Betty laughed. 'That too,' she said.

Kate pulled a wobbly round wooden table towards the bench where they were to sit. It was an old bench, mossy and not very clean; she gave it a cursory wipe with her skirt.

The skirt was old, faded and unevenly hemmed. She had put it on in deference to Betty's visit, with the vague idea that a skirt was smarter than trousers. Usually she wore a comfortable old baggy pair, suitable for both gardening and writing. Betty, on the other hand, had dressed down, in what she considered suitable wear for spending a morning in her friend's garden: a pale-green, pleated skirt with an orange silk blouse which perfectly suited her fair skin. As she looked at the flower beds and rose garden, the immaculate lawns with their trim edges, she couldn't help wondering for a moment why Kate didn't give to her own appearance just a fraction of the attention she gave to the garden's.

'What will he do as a PPS?' Kate was asking, as she offered the biscuit tin, which Betty waved away.

'No, thanks. As far as I can make out, he'll be a kind of dogsbody to the Minister. No extra money in it, but it's a first step on the promotion ladder. I'm really not sure what his duties are. I think he just helps the Minister with questions, letters, speeches and that sort of thing. He reckons he'll need more secretarial help – I mean the proper kind of secretary not the parliamentary kind.'

'Chrissie's daughter's looking for a job,' Kate told her. 'Are you sure you won't have a biscuit? I'm on my third and I haven't been travelling like you. Still I was up at six watering the garden. That's Claire, the younger one,' she went on, when Betty had once again rejected the proffered tin. 'She's a very bright girl, degree in psychology. She did a year's teacher training, but decided not to teach and took a secretarial course instead. And she's just finished a computer course.'

'She might be too highly qualified for this job of Colin's.'

'I don't think so. And last time I was over there I got the impression she wanted something a bit unusual. You know, not an ordinary nine-to-five office job.'

'Well, this should suit her – the hours are awful.'

'She still lives at home so she could easily commute from Staines.'

'Thanks for thinking of her. I'll mention it to Colin.'

'You'd like her. She's your sort of person.'

'What does that mean?'

Kate shrugged.

'Stylish. Dresses like you. She's noticeable somehow.'

She looked affectionately at her elegant friend, with her perfect figure, her white, slender fingers, her immaculately painted nails.

'You always look marvellous,' she said. 'I can't think how you do it.'

She spoke without envy, for she felt none. Well, perhaps just a little for that flat stomach. It was years since she'd been able to hold her own in.

'How do you keep it so flat?' she asked, pointing.

Betty looked at her. 'By not having children,' she replied, stonily.

At first Kate thought she was being rebuked for having Daniel and Paulette. Then she realised. She recognised that look from childhood. The pain in Betty's eyes, the defiance that veiled it. She took her hands in hers.

'Oh, Betty, I'm so sorry,' she said.

To her consternation she saw the chin quiver, the lips tremble, the composed face begin to dissolve. She reached out to her. For a moment Betty fought off tears, digging the red nails into her palms, then she fell against her friend and sobbed.

Kate let her cry; it was best. She suspected Betty hadn't admitted her misery to anyone, probably not to that cold fish Colin. How would she herself have felt if she hadn't been able to have them, Daniel and Paulette? How would she have borne it, the bleak emptiness of it?

Betty grew calmer, found a handkerchief, assembled herself, drew away a little.

'They say you don't miss what you've never had,' she said. 'It's not true.'

'Of course it's not true. They say some stupid things, whoever they are.'

'I'm sorry, Kate. I've never broken down before. We're so much on view, you know, and I'm always having to be cheerful among women and their children. And I mustn't worry Colin.'

'You're having investigations and all that?' Kate was vague about what was involved. She had conceived easily.

Betty nodded.

'Oh, Kate, there's so much waiting. You wait for appointments, then you wait for tests and then you wait for the results of tests. Colin had some tests and they were okay. So far they can't find anything wrong with me. Sometimes people just do have a long wait for babies. It's all about waiting and not knowing. It's the not knowing that wears you down and the repeated cycle of hope and disappointment.'

She took a deep, shuddering breath.

'There, I'm better now,' she said and smiled.

It was rather a watery smile, but counted.

'Thanks, Kate,' she said.

'I've done nothing. I wish I could.'

'Oh yes, you have. You've listened and understood.'

'I'll get you some more coffee,' Kate said. She tried to think of what, in the garden, would cheer her friend up. 'And then I'll show you the compost heap,' she promised.

Chapter Thirteen

'I'm off now,' Chrissie said, coming into the kitchen. 'Everything all right, Mrs Rawley?'

'Don't you worry, everything's under control.'

Chrissie smiled; it was the answer she always got. It was very appropriate too. Everything about Mrs Rawley was controlled; it was impossible to imagine her being flustered, doing anything over-adventurous. She was one who lived within her means in every sense.

A compact little woman, she was very neat in her ways. She had been with Chrissie ever since Rosemary was born. She was one of those women who never look really young, indeed look careworn in their youth, but do not age thereafter, as if they had got middle age over before they even reached it.

She dressed in greys and browns. Today it was the turn of the brown suit with the lighter brown blouse. Claire, sitting next to her at the table as they drank coffee together, was a parakeet beside a house sparrow.

Claire had taken to power dressing since she started work with Colin. This morning she was vivid in purple and orange stripes with shoulders padded like an American football player. Sometimes she twisted her hair into a French pleat in an effort to look more sophisticated, but today it was spread loose about her shoulders, framing a face which still looked challengingly out at the world, almost as if expecting disapproval and defying it in advance.

Why does she feel like this? Chrissie often asked herself. She's always been loved and supported, why should she be so defensive? Was she like this at work? she sometimes wondered. From the way she spoke of her employer and his colleagues, she rather thought not. Perhaps this aggressiveness, this need to be critical, was reserved for her nearest and dearest? Chrissie hoped so, but all the same she couldn't help wondering where it came from, this characteristic of her younger daughter. Was there some underlying lack of security and, if so, why? As she had raked their faces for signs of anything amiss when they were little, so Chrissie now raked her own memory and conscience for signs of where she might perhaps have gone wrong.

'I've just been trying to persuade Mrs Rawley to buy her council house,' Claire said.

'Oh, well, I don't know about that . . .'

Chrissie hesitated. She could hardly say in front of Mrs Rawley that her husband's wages as a hospital porter might not make it easy to support home ownership. Instead she had to make do with giving her daughter a warning look, before she kissed her and left home.

'You see, Mrs Rawley,' Claire went on, after her mother had gone out. 'It's always sensible to borrow long and lend short. Now I don't know what you pay for rent for your house, but suppose it was thirty pounds a week and instead you put that towards a mortgage of say twenty thousand—'

Mrs Rawley shook her head.

'There's no way we'd go borrowing that kind of money,' she said. 'I'd never sleep easy of a night.'

'No, listen. Instead of paying rent, you'd pay interest on your loan and gradually pay off the capital until you owned the place. And you could sell it again if you wanted to.'

Mrs Rawley only shook her head again and smiled. She just wasn't taking any of this seriously.

'Honestly. There are people who've bought their council houses and sold them for double the money two years later. Think of that.'

'There's someone near us who did that. He bought a race horse with the money and lost everything. He's homeless now, back on the council waiting list. It's all right for some, Claire, but not for others. It wouldn't do for the likes of us.'

'But you're far too sensible to go buying race horses, Mrs Rawley.'

They both laughed at the very idea.

'No, it's kind of you to think of it for us, but you see we manage very nicely now. My husband's wages pay for the rent and gas and electric. And what I earn here pays for food and clothes. We get along very well.'

'But you could do better. That's the point. Everyone should want to better themselves.'

'We have bettered ourselves,' Mrs Rawley said quietly. 'And now, if you'll excuse me, I must get on with my work.'

'And goodness, I must get off to my assertiveness class.'

At the doorway she turned back and said, 'But don't forget about the house business. I'm sure it would be great for you.'

'Then we'll have to disagree about it, won't we? And really it's Mr Rawley you should talk to. He's the one who pays the rent.'

'That's a good idea. I'll talk to him. I'm sure he'd understand. We'll fix a time later. But I must be off now.'

Mrs Rawley stood for a moment, surprised that she had somehow come to an arrangement for Claire to talk to her husband. She really was a one, that girl was, she reflected, shaking her head, as she began to clear the dishes into the sink. And ever since she'd started working for that MP it had been Colin this and Colin that. And anyone less in need of going to assertiveness classes she couldn't imagine.

Chrissie sat in the lecture room at the hospital and tried to concentrate on what the man was saying.

Her mind kept wandering off, imagining what was going on in the ward. They had been so overstretched yesterday. The trouble was that she couldn't see the point of most of what the lecturer was on about. Cost effectiveness, he kept repeating. He wanted them all to be making a contribution towards it. Chrissie couldn't think what contribution she could possibly make towards it, whatever it was. Her contribution was nursing. That's why she'd gone in for it, what she had wanted to do all her life. It really hurt her to be taken off the ward for this study day, away from the patients.

Tendering, accountability, the internal market, the unfamiliar words floated over her. Determinedly, she took notes, hoping Jack would make some sense of it for her tonight. Glancing about, she was relieved to see that her fellow-nurses were looking similarly bemused.

The afternoon's lecture left her as bewildered as the morning's. The lecturer wanted them all to be involved, he said. It was essential that they all understood how the funds were managed, he kept emphasising. If she'd wanted to understand about funds,

Chrissie thought with unaccustomed rancour, she'd have trained as an accountant in the first place.

'It isn't as if you're committing yourself to anything, Mr Rawley,' Claire said. 'Just go along and talk to him, find out a few facts. There's no harm in that, is there?'

She leant forward as she spoke, her expression eager, helpful, her mass of golden hair bright against the grey moquette of the three-piece suite. The Rawleys sat opposite to her, side by side on the couch, attentive and wary.

'There's harm if one thing leads to another,' Janet Rawley pointed out.

'But it's very good of you to take so much trouble,' Geoff said, in unconscious apology for his wife's brusqueness.

He was impressed by Claire, Janet could see that: it wasn't difficult to read his big, open countenance. She could tell that he wanted to oblige Claire, didn't want to seem ungrateful.

'They're very good houses on the Barrow Court estate,' Claire was saying. 'Everyone says they're well built.'

Janet knew that; she didn't need Claire to come and tell her. The houses had been built before the war, on the edge of the town, more a village really in those days. They'd cost three hundred pounds each to build and her parents rented one after the war for a pound a week. She'd been born in that house, gone to school from it, done her homework in the front room.

They'd paid for themselves many times over, those houses had, and the council had used the money to build new ones and improve the old.

It was in one of the new houses, on the same estate, that she and Geoff had begun their married life and lived there ever since, not far away from the house where she was born.

'Oh, they're very good houses,' Geoff agreed. 'And built to higher specifications than the old ones.'

He knew something about the building trade, did Geoff. He'd been in it himself until the cuts of the early Eighties put him out of work. He'd been lucky; he'd managed to get a job as a porter in the local hospital. But he didn't need Claire to tell him whether a house was well built or not.

'So you see, Mr Rawley, this house would be a very good investment,' Claire went on.

'This is our home,' Janet told her. 'We don't see it as an investment.'

'Oh, but you should. For most people their home is their greatest asset.'

'And a great expense,' Janet told her.

She turned towards Geoff, on the couch beside her.

'When there's tiles off the roof or trouble with the chimney, there'd be no ringing up the council.'

'Yes, but some of the things I could fix myself.'

'But not all. And then there'd be the materials to buy. And it might come at a bad time. You know where you are with the rent.'

'Yes, it's regular like, is the rent.'

'Buying a house isn't for the likes of us,' Janet summed up.

'Oh, Mrs Rawley,' Claire exclaimed. 'That's quite the wrong attitude. As my boss always says, we live in a property-owning democracy.'

'Well, let's say we'll think about it,' Geoff said, placating disapproval. 'We've got the card, thank you, so we can go and see the gentleman at the council any time – without committing ourselves to anything, of course,' he added hastily.

'Yes, he is expecting you,' Claire said, getting up to leave. And she shook his hand, as if somehow sealing a bargain.

'It's really good of her,' Geoff said, after she'd left. He stood for a moment looking at the card, a small thing in his big hand, then, 'I think we should go and see this gentleman, Janet,' he said. 'Just to show our appreciation of what she's done. It's very kind of her to trouble herself about us.'

Janet said nothing. Instinct told her that Claire was not acting out of kindness. Maybe she was gratifying some need to interfere, maybe she just wanted to please that boss of hers. She didn't really know what Claire's motive was. But she knew what it wasn't.

Chapter Fourteen

Betty wore the red dress for the housewarming. Made of fine velvet and clinging, it was a spectacular garment. What Colin had objected to was the colour.

'Couldn't you get it in blue?' he had asked, when she lifted it out of its tissue paper the week before. 'I mean, red isn't exactly appropriate, is it?'

She laughed at him.

'It hadn't occurred to me that I was to wear the party flag,' she said, stepping into the dress. 'And I didn't *get* it. I had it made. Can you do me up?'

She leant against him and he pulled up the long zip at the back.

'Flagpole is what I am not,' she said, moving away from him.

She walked about the room, turning so that he could see the dress from all angles and yes, he had to admit it was stunning.

'It would have looked nothing in blue,' she told him. 'And next to you in black this colour will be marvellous. Besides, it isn't as if it's a political do. It's our *home* that we're warming; we're not opening a branch office of party headquarters.'

'The majority of our guests will be colleagues and supporters—'

'Don't forget all *my* old colleagues from work and friends like Kate and Luke, Chrissie and Jack, and Nell and lots of locals who couldn't care less about politics.'

'Everyone should care about politics,' he corrected her.

Sometimes nowadays he addressed her like a public meeting, she thought. She really must stop him getting pompous: that is one of a wife's duties, which should be incorporated into the marriage service.

'There are people, Colin,' she told him, wrapping her arms around his neck and punctuating each phrase with a kiss, 'for whom party politics is just a necessary evil, a game which they themselves don't think worth giving time to. They care much more about their work, their children, about reading, theatre and their hobbies than about who's in and who's out.'

'But—'

'But me no buts,' she told him, kissing him again. 'The occupational hazard of politicians is arrogance and getting out of touch with the real world. Watch it!'

He knew there was sense in her words. If anyone else had spoken them he would probably have agreed, but it seemed to him that these weren't the words that should issue from the mouth of an ambitious young politician's wife. She should be urging him on, not issuing warnings, he thought petulantly.

'You see, darling,' she was saying, 'if politics becomes an insider's game, people aren't going to bother to watch it, let alone join in. Aren't you lucky to have a wife who'll tell you these things?' she added laughing, and pressing herself against him.

Oh, yes he was lucky. He knew that. He had been right when he had calculated that she would make a good political wife. She was at ease with everyone, they all liked her. She seemed to have the common touch with the mass of supporters and waverers, yet the hierarchy found her good and witty company. A wife for all seasons, Betty was, he thought as, all petulance forgotten, he gave himself up to kissing her and the world swam into place.

And now, as he waited for the guests to arrive, he thought again how lucky he was to have her as his consort. He'd got ready far too early and was stuck in that limbo between the rush of preparation and the excitement of the guests arriving, when time stands still and everything seems unnaturally tidy, untouched.

It had all been his idea, this impressive housewarming, but now he almost regretted it as he stood in the hall, suddenly nervous in his grand house, looking at his watch and dreading that something would go spectacularly wrong.

But there was Betty, confident and calm, relishing every moment as she chatted to the caterers, checking details, seeing to everything.

'It's just a matter of making lists,' she told him airily. 'Why are you looking so worried? If the wind changes you'll be stuck with that frown. That's what Mrs Hough used to tell us.'

Suddenly he grabbed her and kissed her hard.

'Oh, thank God for you,' he said, to her astonishment, as

she heard the sound of the first car scrunching on the gravel.

Then they were all arriving, the house quickly filling with talk and laughter, introductions being made, food and drink and guests all circulating, the waiters carrying out instructions to the letter. Fully occupied himself now, he could yet observe Betty moving in that brilliant dress from group to group, leaving behind her a trail of laughter and goodwill, patently enjoying herself. She wasn't anxious, as he was; she happily introduced to each other, people whom he would have sweated to keep apart.

There was Nell, for example, talking to the Minister.

'I learned my lesson last time,' the Minister was saying. 'I'm against all public spending now. If people want things, they should pay for them themselves.'

'You remind me of the story about Winston Churchill. When he was a Liberal Member he was speaking at a public meeting before an election and a not particularly clean old man kept asking, "Why should I pay the education rate when I don't have any children?" After a lot of these interruptions, Churchill snarled back, "For the same reason that you pay water rates and don't wash."'

Colin cringed. Oh God, he shouldn't have let Betty invite her. He'd apologise to the Minister afterwards.

But the Minister was laughing.

'Touché,' he said.

Later he asked Colin who that handsome woman was. He'd like to meet her again, very intelligent and well-informed, he thought her. Very stimulating to talk to. So instead of an apology, Colin found himself having to offer an address.

Betty had wanted to place people at their separate tables for dinner so that she could mix them all up, but this Colin had resisted.

'Let them choose where they'll sit,' he said and she had agreed that it would be more informal.

It turned out as he had hoped; people tended to sit with their own kind. It was safer so.

Thus it was that, as he stood by the fireplace, looking to see which table he should join, he found himself near a group of people he thought of as the country gentry, friends of the former owner whose family had lived here for generations.

'It always used to be so cold in this house,' one of them was saying loudly to another. 'Whenever we came we used to put on thermal underwear and wear woolly dresses.'

'Yes, and stand as close to the fire as we decently could.'

'And the agony of having to leave it and go into that icy dining room.'

'It was like walking into a refrigerator.'

'Yes, even the chairs struck cold when you sat on them.'

There was laughter. Then, 'It's so different now. Unbelievable. What a difference it makes when *money* takes over a house.'

'Yes, family is all very well, but it's money that installs the central heating.'

They were loud-voiced, these county people. Colin clenched his fists as he heard them.

'Somebody said he'd bought the portraits of the ancestors, but I don't see them, do you?'

'Calumny, dear. They were sold to pay off death duties.'

Rage and shame filled him. Who did they think they were to be so condescending? What had any of them ever done? He must get a grip on himself. How would Betty handle it? He tried hard to imagine. She would probably tell him that they had done something; they had voted for him.

He walked across to the table.

'May I join you?' he asked, consciously suave, as he drew up a chair.

They welcomed him, they fêted him, they asked how the session was going, he was their man. He began to relax. They were all right, he must perhaps just try to be more like them.

'Colin,' the Deputy Chairman of the local party was saying, 'I know this isn't the time to talk business, but since we have you to ourselves for a moment, perhaps I could just tell you that some members of the Association think that we should increase the heating grants to pensioners next winter.'

Remembering that he must try to be more like them, he replied facetiously, 'Tell them that with all this global warming, old age pensioners can forget about their hypothermia.'

To his surprise they looked at him with distaste. There's simply no pleasing some of these people, he thought, and, shortly afterwards, moved on.

He and Betty led the dancing. By now the wine and good food had done their work. Soon nearly everyone was dancing and those who weren't were sitting around in friendly groups, chatting. The Chairman of the Association had a gammy leg. Colin asked his wife to dance. After Betty, she was certainly the most elegantly dressed and coiffed woman in the room. As they moved on to the floor, Luke danced past with Kate, who, it seemed to Colin, was perhaps the least elegantly dressed woman in the room.

He saw that his partner was watching her, her expression amused.

'An old school friend of my wife's,' he said, to explain her presence.

'Yes, I've been talking to her. A delightful soul and so knowledgeable about my obsession.'

'Which is?'

'Gardening. I've spent a fortune having these compost boxes made and it still doesn't work. But she's explained the whole thing. I'm going to go and see her next month. I mean she really does get the compost down to the friable mixture the books talk about. Texture of Christmas pudding, it should be, you know. Or did she say cake?'

For the whole of the dance she talked about pruning and greenfly, or so it seemed to Colin, who had been hoping for informed gossip about local politics.

They danced the last waltz together, he and Betty, cheek to cheek. Then they stood in the centre of the room while their guests stood in a great circle around them singing 'For He's a Jolly Good Fellow', and it was all very touching.

'Happy with the way it went?' Betty asked after they had said the last farewell, accepted the last thanks, heard the last car drive away. She was sitting on the stairs, leaning against the banisters. Suddenly weary, he sat down beside her.

'I must say I enjoyed it much more than I expected,' she went on. 'There's so much hassle beforehand that it comes as quite a surprise to have so much fun when it actually happens, doesn't it?'

'That's true,' he said, yawning and wondering how she could be so wide-awake and talkative, when he himself felt so drained.

'The caterers have been marvellous,' she was saying, 'and the band too. There really won't be much mess to clear up tomorrow.'

She hesitated. 'You did enjoy it, didn't you?' she asked.

'Oh yes, yes, of course. It went very well.'

'You just sound a bit less than enthusiastic. Anything wrong?'

He couldn't tell her about the overheard conversation. He couldn't tell her about his vague suspicion that they all got on better with each other than they did with him. He couldn't tell her that at times he had felt less like a host, more like an outsider.

Instead, 'We need a night cap,' he said, and poured them each a brandy.

'Lots of people told me what a good MP they thought you were,' she said, raising her glass to him. 'They're really proud of you. And so they should be. You work very hard for them.'

She put down her glass and kissed him and he felt all his old confidence return. He'd been tired, he told himself, that's all it was. It had passed already, that feeling of let-down, that sometimes comes after a party, even such a successful one as this.

'Thank you, Betty,' he said, 'for making it such a wonderful housewarming. It's the sort of thing that will do my career a lot of good.'

'Oh, Colin! You mustn't see everything in terms of work and career.'

'I'm ashamed to say,' he told her, as they sat on the stairs drinking their brandy, 'that we politicians are very competitive animals. It's a rat race we're involved in and we love it.'

'But even if you win,' she demurred, 'you're still only a rat.'

Chapter Fifteen

'This calls for a housewarming, this does,' Geoff Rawley said, putting the bottle of celebration sherry on the kitchen table. 'Everything signed and sealed, as they say.'

He hesitated and then went on, 'Do you think we could ask the Pilkingtons round?'

His wife believed in keeping themselves to themselves, but the Pilkingtons were their neighbours and were occasionally invited.

'Could do,' she reluctantly agreed. 'Since it's Friday. I'll send our Brian round with a note.'

'My, but it's a tiring business, buying a house,' Geoff said, as they both sat down on the couch, exhausted.

'I'll make a pot of tea,' she said, getting up. 'We could do with it.'

Gradually the tea revived them.

'All ours, Janet,' Geoff said, looking around him in wonder. 'It's hard to believe.'

It was true; the place looked different now that they owned it. The furniture looked better somehow: the three-piece suite, the pinewood dining room table with matching chairs, which they had saved up for years to buy, not wanting anything on the never-never, and the bookcase, which Geoff had made so that Janet would have somewhere to put the ornaments, all looked more in keeping with this house now that they owned it. Even the brasses on the fireplace seemed to gleam more brightly.

'Let's have a look round,' Geoff suggested and, although she shook her head at him, she smiled tolerantly as she allowed him to lead her round the familiar rooms, up the same old stairs, but looking at everything with new eyes, eyes bright with the pride of possession.

'Susan's bedroom,' he said, looking at the neat and tidy room, with the pink floral wallpaper, which his daughter had chosen when he had decorated it for her last year, and the matching curtains and bedspread which Janet had made.

'Brian's room,' she said next. 'And I doubt if he'll be much tidier now that it's our own. It won't make any difference to him who owns the house, I'll be bound.'

Oh yes, she still had her doubts. Time would tell. The officer had been very courteous; when they'd explained that they'd really just come to find out a bit more and didn't want to commit themselves, he'd seemed a bit disappointed in them, which made Geoff apologetic. Their arguments began to sound like excuses.

'Do you really want to go on paying rent all your life and have nothing at the end to show for it, when you could pay a mortgage instead and have a house of your own, something to leave to your children at the end of the day?' he'd asked in tones of disbelief.

It was the argument about the children that persuaded Geoff. She knew it would; he'd do anything for the children. She sensed there was a flaw in the argument somewhere, that the officer was speaking the language of another tribe, but all the certainty seemed to be on his side and all the uncertainty on theirs. In the end they agreed. Then the officer and his assistants were all over Geoff, making him feel like one of them, somehow.

They were in the fashion, of course. Others were doing the same, which was reassuring; it was like swimming with the tide. People were queueing up to buy council houses, the Minister said; they'd seen him almost dancing for joy on the television last week. 'It's the sale of the century,' proclaimed the rejoicing Minister.

'If he put his own house up for sale at half its value, people would no doubt queue up to buy it,' Janet had pointed out. 'But he wouldn't, would he? It would be his own money then. But these houses he's selling belong to the ratepayers and he doesn't mind losing their money.'

Oh, yes, she had always been the more doubting of the two of them, the more suspicious of the whole business.

Well, it was done now, she told herself, as she and Geoff came downstairs, and she certainly wasn't going to spoil his first evening of being a householder by carping on about it. Better just tidy up the sitting room and then get herself into her best dress ready for the guests. It was the only brightly coloured garment she possessed. It was blue and she used to say she'd chosen it to show the colour of her politics.

Brian and Susan were allowed a sip of sherry because it was a special occasion. The Pilkingtons brought a box of chocolates and the four adults made polite conversation as they always did when visiting each other's homes. They drank a toast to the house and Geoff made a short speech. Then the children were allowed out and the grown-ups sat on, talking in a more relaxed manner now, as they ate the chocolates and drank the sweet sherry.

Chapter Sixteen

'Good luck with your speech,' Betty had said again, before she rang off, 'I'll be with you in spirit.'

As if that made up for being absent in the flesh, Colin reflected sourly, as he put the receiver down. He hadn't realised until then how much he had been hoping that she'd cancel her appointment and turn up at the last minute, just in time to hear his speech. It was the first speech he had made from the platform, his first ever as a Junior Minister.

It had been bad enough writing the damned thing on his own. It was the first time he'd composed a speech like this without her help. He'd missed her badly; she had such a neat turn of phrase, came up with some splendid one-liners. They worked well together, he supplied the meat and she the spice; that was how he put it.

This time he'd consulted Claire once or twice about the odd awkward paragraph, but her ideas had been quite hopeless; it brought home to him how good Betty was at this sort of thing.

It had gone off all right in the end; the leader had approved. But there was a hollowness in him as he acknowledged the applause. He wanted his wife there to share his success. He needed her in bed afterwards.

Of course, no wife was obliged to come, year in, year out, but dammit, this year was very special. It was the first conference since the 1987 election and triumph was in the air. The leader had smiled at him three times and had addressed those few thrilling words of congratulation to him after his speech. His wife just *ought* to have been there. Of course Betty had never pretended to enjoy these junketings and he had a suspicion that she didn't much care for some of his colleagues. Well, neither did he, come to that. She hadn't said so outright, just that she had to be in London for these tests. The time of the month was evidently crucially important. Or so she said.

Frankly, he was getting a bit fed up with this baby business. In his view, Betty was getting obsessed by it. After all, everybody knew that the world was over-populated, so why add to the world's problems? If politicians couldn't take a global view, how could they expect others to do so?

Of course he understood that she must sometimes be lonely in that great house when he was in London; she couldn't drop everything just to be with him, as she had done in the early days. In his view, a dog was the answer. Better still, a pair of dogs. Something big. Dobermann pinschers were the fashionable breed just now. He could imagine them gracing the grounds of the manor house, protecting his estate while he was away.

He smiled as he imagined it, pleased with the picture of those great dogs protecting the estates of their absent master. It befitted his image so much better than a pramful of baby, a vision more suited to some suburban back garden.

Claire was here, of course, and the next best thing to having an enviable wife alongside him was to have an enviable secretary. Colin needed the envy of his fellow man. Certainly his fellow MPs envied him his stunning secretary. Claire had blossomed since she first came to work for him. She had always been an attractive girl but now that she had let her hair grow into a great golden mass of thick waves and curls, she looked stunning. There was an ambiguity about her face – and about her too, strange creature that she was. Most women with such perfect looks would have had a certain self-awareness. Claire seemed strangely unaware of her charms. When others might flirt, she would discuss in a serious, almost pedantic way. There was still something of the earnest sixth-former about her. It was an unsophisticated face, innocent of make-up, and there was often a puzzled, questioning look in the huge, dark eyes, made to seem darker by those amazing long black lashes. Men were intrigued by her.

After having tea with her, one of his colleagues had once asked Colin how he could endure hearing all that women's lib stuff issuing forth from between those delicious lips. 'It would be more than my flesh and blood could stand,' he'd said. 'I'd just have to stop them with my own.'

Colin remembered the remark with satisfaction, glad that he had with him the kind of girl other men wanted. Not that there'd be any hanky-panky, nothing like that. He wasn't that sort of a man and anyway she had a boyfriend. But it was good to have her lovely presence here, applauding his speech, ministering to his needs, taking him very seriously, being a cause of envy in his colleagues.

It was six o'clock. He made his way to the bar, postponing the time he would have to return to the hotel for his lonely dinner.

'Join you?'

He didn't need to turn in his chair to recognise the clipped tones of the member for Flaxton West, the constituency adjoining his own. Frankly rather a vulgar man, but entertaining in his way. He waved towards the chair opposite.

'Congrats on the speech, old man. It went down a treat.'

'Thank you. Yes, the audience was very kind,' Colin said modestly. 'I tried to say all the things which need saying.'

The MP for Flaxton West shrugged. 'Oh, they don't give a monkey's what you say,' he replied. 'It's how you say it and what you look like when you say it, that counts. If I'd made your speech, tubby old frump that I am, they'd hardly have given it a yawn, but an Adonis like you can get away with every cliché in the book and they'll get up and ovate like any old thing. Take it from me, old chap, I've seen it, year in, year out. You are of the Darling of Conference variety. I'm not complaining. Make the most of it. I would in your shoes.'

'How about joining me for dinner tonight?' Colin suggested, after they had talked for a while.

'Sorry. No can do. I'm wining and dining ten of my constituents tonight,' he said. 'Have to reward the party faithful on these occasions, you know. Sorry, old man.'

'That's all right. I understand. I did my lot last night.'

'Of course, you're on your tod, aren't you? I saw Betty wasn't here.'

'No, she had to be in London. I might ask Peters; he's on his own too.'

The Member for Flaxton West laughed.

'I shouldn't do that,' he said. 'He's got his secretary with him. They're nicely shacked up in a discreet little hotel outside town.'

Colin said nothing.

'Don't look so disapproving, old chap,' the other MP went on.

105

'Nobody's really arrived in politics until they've had at least one affair. Everyone knows that.'

Colin shook his head, but the seed had been planted; after they had parted, he pondered what the other man had said. So it was acceptable to have an affair, obligatory even. Here was another social rule to be learned. He had been born into a narrow, puritanical little world, he reflected, as he remembered his mother's ferocious respectability. Step by step he had abandoned its ways and copied the manners of those whom he would once have thought his betters. Perhaps the final adaptation he had to make was a moral one. He must not, he thought as he left the bar, give away his origins by displaying signs of lower middle class morality.

He walked back to the hotel by a roundabout route. He felt restless, still elated by the success of his speech. The Blackpool air was crisp, exhilarating. He took deep breaths of it. He was filled with a sense of animal well-being. I'm thirty-nine, in my prime, he thought as he strode along. Only one term as an MP and he'd increased his majority by three thousand, been the first of the new intake to be appointed PPS and now about to be Minister of State. He was one to watch, some people were already saying. He'd have his own PPS now. Maybe Claire would need an assistant, he thought suddenly, as he saw his little coterie growing, revolving round him, all people who would look to him as the source of their power. He felt the potent force of it.

He came down to earth as he entered the hotel. The lobby was almost deserted, just a few of the staff hanging about. People would be getting ready for an evening out, in their pairs they would be. Again he thought longingly of Betty, all those miles away.

He nearly bumped into a girl coming out of the lift. He apologised, saw it was Claire.

'Oh, I'm so pleased to see you,' she said. 'I was sorry to miss you earlier. I did want to say that your speech was great, really great.'

'Thank you. And thank you for your help with it.'

'You didn't look at the notes once,' she pointed out.

'Ah, but I knew that they were there. Very reassuring. Well, I mustn't delay you. I expect you're on your way out.'

'No, I just came down to post a card. My little sister Rosemary loves to get picture postcards.'

She held it up to show him: a picture of the sea, with a message carefully printed in big capital letters.

He found it rather touching.

'It's very sweet of you,' he said, 'to remember your little sister when you've so much else to think about here.'

She shrugged.

'Oh, I've nothing much to do at the moment,' she said. 'I was just going to look around for somewhere to eat.'

'We can't have that,' he said on an impulse. 'Have dinner with me tonight. You deserve a bit of spoiling after all your hard work.'

'Oh, I'd love to.'

She was blushing with pleasure, like a child, yet so gloriously a woman.

'Do you mean here, at the hotel?'

He hesitated. The seed which had been planted earlier began to grow, to put out shoots of tenderness.

'Yes, but the dining room isn't up to much. I'll have dinner sent up to my room. The room service is excellent. Much better than in the dining room,' he added.

She accepted the reason. Had she not also observed how slow the service was in the dining room?

Colin's room was small but elegant. It was not unfamiliar to her, for she had worked with him on his speech here, but now, softly lit and the papers tidied away, it seemed much cosier. A bottle of champagne stood in a silver bucket on the coffee table. She watched as he expertly opened it.

'I've never had champagne except once at a wedding,' she remarked.

'Do you know, Claire, there's more champagne drunk in England now per head of population than ever before in our history? We drink more per capita even than the French?'

'Really?' she breathed, deeply impressed.

'Yes, a third of a bottle per head when you average it out. *And* consumption's up by seven per cent this year. It says a lot for what we've done for Britain,' he went on, 'when you realise that we imported three hundred thousand hectolitres of champagne this year compared to a mere hundred and seventy thousand when we came to power.'

107

Claire listened, impressed. It was amazing the way these statistics came out, and they were always so favourable. He talked on and she thought what a contrast he was with her father. Dad knew a lot, of course, but it was about things like buildings and engineering, not important things like the consumption of champagne. And he looked so distinguished; she could sometimes hardly believe that she, Claire, actually worked for such a man. This reminded her that she had a worry.

'When you take up your new post, I mean now that you're a Junior Minister, shall I still be your secretary?'

'But of course,' he assured her. 'I'll need you more than ever.'

He stopped suddenly, looked at her, then went on, 'Claire, I'm so sorry. Have you been anxious about this? How thoughtless of me! I do apologise. I should have made it quite clear from the start.'

Colin had a way with profuse apology that made the recipient feel even more beholden. Claire hardly knew what to say to stop him feeling so guilty.

'Oh, *please*. I mean, it's quite all right. It was stupid of me but it was just that I – I mean, well, you mustn't apologise.'

Jack and Chrissie would scarcely have recognised this stammering girl as their daughter, so assured with them, so uncertain of herself with her employer.

'That's very sweet of you,' Colin was saying, 'but I was in the wrong.'

'I just thought, you know, that you might want someone more experienced, older and everything.'

He took her hand, looked reassuringly into her eyes, those huge luminous eyes, with their extraordinarily long lashes, which looked out at the world with unexpected naivety, innocence even. Certainly this look prevailed now that she was confused.

'I'll need your help more than ever now,' he told her again warmly, as he continued to look into those eyes.

She gazed back, thrilled and flattered, but was saved having to think of a reply by a knock at the door.

The waiter pushed in the dinner trolley. He steered it into the centre of the room, expertly raised a flap at each side to make a big round table, over which he spread a crisp white damask tablecloth and proceeded to arrange silverware, cut glass, china and thick linen table napkins. In the centre was a heavy metal hotplate laden with covered dishes. He placed a second bottle in a cooler on the side table, alongside puddings and cheese.

To Claire it was like something on a film set.

She watched the waiter's every move, until he stood back and asked Colin, 'Is everything in order, sir?'

Colin nodded.

'Perhaps you could be so good as to put the trolley outside the door when you've finished, sir?' he asked, adding, 'Then l shan't need to disturb you.'

As Colin drew back a chair for her, Claire almost had to pinch herself. What would her sister think if she could see her now? Poor old Sarah, with her school dinners.

She spoke little, just nodding and making the odd comment as Colin talked of ministers and world affairs and likely economic outcomes and she ate venison pâté and duckling à l'orange and unfamiliar vegetables and drank a great deal. In fact she had an awful feeling that she was drinking more than he was, he was so generous in filling up her glass in preference to his own.

As he talked she felt increasingly excited at the idea of being so close to the centre of power, here where decisions were made which would affect everyone in the country and he was talking to her as if to an equal. Perhaps, she thought, she deserved to be fêted a little because she had played her small role, serving her master. She began to think her contribution must have been greater than she'd realised, otherwise why should she be so honoured? She had made one or two suggestions about the speech, perhaps that was it. She glowed at the thought, positively glowed.

Colin watched her, he observed that glow, observed the brightness of her eye, observed how relaxed her body was. Oh yes, the body language was very encouraging. He would get rid of the table, they would move over to the comfortable chairs to have their liqueurs. The bed was huge.

'I'll get rid of this clutter,' he suggested, indicating the remains of their meal. 'Then we can relax.'

She made a vague attempt to help, but he waved her aside.

'My turn to wait on you,' he said, smiling down at her.

So she watched as he moved all the dishes off the flap on one side of the table and prepared to lower it.

There was a wooden arm with a ring supporting the flap. He tried – and failed – to push it in.

'Something's stuck,' he said, peering under the flap. 'I'll have to get underneath.'

He bent under the table, pushing at the protruding arm which obstinately refused to budge. Annoyed, he lay right down on his back to get a better leverage and at last felt the thing begin to move. Slowly he pushed the wooden arm back into its groove and the flap began to descend.

Then, to his astonishment, a bread roll flew past his ear. Two plates followed and then a dish of butter, which skidded and smeared its way across the carpet, leaving a shiny, yellow trail in its wake. Two tumblers followed and smashed beside him, followed by an assortment of knives and forks. Wine glasses, side plates and a sugar dredger now cascaded down, followed by a pair of salt and pepper pots. Then the tablecloth began its slow descent, dragging everything else down with it, including the heavy iron hotplate, which missed the side of his head by millimetres. As everything else smashed down on to the floor all round him, he lay still, waiting for the bombardment to cease, totally bewildered by this swift change of scene.

At last it was silent. Very carefully, avoiding putting his hands on pieces of broken glass, Colin raised himself. All around him were strewn knives and forks, dishes, broken glasses, a few bones and bits of assorted vegetables. The contents of salt and pepper pots, sauce boats, cream jugs and sugar basins were spread across the carpet. Raising himself on one arm, still partly under the table, Colin surveyed the scene; it looked like a Roman orgy.

Claire was standing, stricken.

'I was trying to help,' she said.

'What the hell did you do?'

'I thought you couldn't move the flap, so when you went under the table I thought you must be trying to move the one on the other side, so I moved all the things over.'

'But didn't you see what was happening?'

She nodded, the great eyes full of tears.

'I was so surprised,' she said. 'I just couldn't move.'

'Well, it's no good crying,' Colin told her brusquely. 'We'd better just clear up what we can and then ring for the maid.'

But Claire wasn't crying. She was trying so hard not to laugh that her eyes kept filling up. If only he knew how funny he looked sitting there in the sea of broken china and bits of food. There was a prawn in his ear.

Chapter Seventeen

Colin was an only child. Growing up without any teasing siblings and with elderly, earnest parents, he was unused to mockery and couldn't endure it as an adult. So although he had got Claire out of the room as quickly as he decently could, the memory of her unexpected mirth haunted him thereafter. If only he could have laughed with her, everything might have been different. As it was, for days afterwards it returned to him, the sight of this beautiful girl heaving with suppressed mirth as he lay there among the scattered remains of their dinner, and he would feel his stomach tighten with humiliation. Every time he looked at her in the office, he saw her as she had been that night and each time it became clearer to him that the only way he could expiate his humiliation was to have her, as he should have done that night. He must have her groaning and imploring. He must be the one who looked down and smiled. That was the new picture he would superimpose on the old.

He was angry with himself, too, for grovelling about like that on the floor. With hindsight he realised that a gentleman who has trouble with a piece of hotel furniture should ring for a servant to see to it. He should not try to mend it with his own hands. Certainly he should not crawl about under tables. The episode had revealed to him yet another lack in his upbringing and he sweated as he remembered it.

For Claire, too, they were nervous days. She tried not to think about the dreadful way that lovely evening had ended, but she couldn't help remembering, and blushed whenever she did so. It was just too appalling that she'd had a giggling fit, like a silly schoolgirl, when he had so honoured her by inviting her up to dinner. If only he'd referred to it later, made some light-hearted mention or even told her off, she would have known what to do. As it was, she had an awful dread that he would find a reason to sack her, so she worked with even more than her

113

usual willingness, doing his bidding eagerly, while avoiding his eye.

Often she worked late, so was still in the little office she shared with the rest of his staff when Colin rang one evening and asked her to collect some papers and bring them round to his flat.

'Get a taxi, Claire,' he said. 'And bring those two large Manilla envelopes with you. I'd come over myself but I can't leave here, I'm afraid. I've promised to stay and take a call. You don't mind? It might take a couple of hours.'

She didn't mind. Of course she didn't. She'd nothing else arranged for the evening. She'd come immediately.

'I've booked a table at the little restaurant across the square,' he told her when she arrived. 'We'll go over there once you've got all this work out of the way. I hope that suits you?'

Of course it suited her, anything suited her.

'You see, I want to get these letters off urgently. If you can get them down now and process them first thing tomorrow, I'll pop in and sign them at about eleven. Do you think you can manage that?'

Of course she could manage; she was surprised that he was making such an issue of it.

So she sat at the table in his own little sitting room, making notes, pinning letters and answers together, marking passages in a report he wanted to have condensed.

At eight o'clock, just as she was finishing, he brought her jacket and draped it around her shoulders.

'I'm starving, if you're not,' he said, keeping his hands resting on her shoulders with a gentle pressure. She felt a tremor of pleasure and instinctively pressed her shoulders back against his hands.

'Leave the papers here,' he said. 'We'll come back and get them after dinner. Then we'll find a taxi to take you home.'

'A *taxi*? Wouldn't that be awfully expensive?'

'You'll have earned it,' he foretold.

So she left the papers on the table, collected her bag and followed him out into the street.

It was a summer evening, sultry and sweet-scented under the lime trees in the little park, which they had to cross to reach the far side of the square. A few children were playing; one was bowling a hoop.

'I haven't seen one of those for a long time,' Colin remarked, suddenly remembering the mean street in which he had bowled an old metal hoop years ago, his mother peering anxiously out of the net curtains to make sure he wasn't playing with any of the rough boys. He hated the way these memories came unbidden to his mind. He clenched his fists for a moment, thought of the girl laughing at him. Then, angry with himself, he put the picture out of his mind, and, reminding himself of who he was now, how he lived now, he took a firm grip on his companion's arm.

'We'll cross here,' he commanded and steered her across the road and into the restaurant.

For an awful moment, as the proprietor approached with a professional smile of welcome, he thought the man might ask after Betty. Perhaps professional tact prevailed, or perhaps it was just chance, but nothing was said. Unaware, Claire followed her master to the corner table.

Red prevailed in the decor at Fatio's; tablecloths, wallpaper, lampshades, were all red, suffusing everything in a pinkish glow. 'It's so pretty,' she exclaimed, looking about her, wide-eyed, and he smiled back at her benignly, as a father might at a child appreciative of the treat he is giving it. He helped her with the choice of dishes, wine flowed, she relaxed, she felt woman-of-the-worldish, sophisticated, as if she too was wrapped in a pinkish glow. She was amazed when he said, 'Nearly eleven o'clock, time to go back and pick up all the bits and pieces and speed you on your way home in a taxi.'

'It's been a lovely evening, thank you,' she said, suddenly childish again.

It was dark now, but the night air was still warm and sultry. A noisy group of youths, gathered at the corner of the park, provided an excuse for him to take her arm and keep it firmly in his. She could feel the pressure of his arm against her side and the tingling of the wine in her veins.

'We'll have a quick night cap,' he said, 'after you've put the papers together.'

He had a brandy and poured her a liqueur. It was sweet and strong, so strong that she almost pulled a face at the first mouthful, but after that it was lovely. He refilled her glass.

This he decided was the moment to mention the unmentionable. 'You know, Claire,' he began, 'I do owe you an apology for

115

spoiling your evening at the hotel with my clumsiness. I've been meaning to apologise for so long, but you know how busy I've been and there are always so many people around.'

She reacted as he'd expected. She flushed, she was flustered.

'Oh,' she said, reaching out her hands, 'you mustn't apologise; it was all my fault.'

He took her outstretched hands in his own.

'No, it was my fault,' he insisted, 'and I was perhaps a little short afterwards. Am I forgiven?'

He looked appealingly at her, this handsome boss of hers, his head on one side, one eyebrow slightly raised.

'But, of course.'

'Seal it?' he interrupted.

It was only a light little kiss, that first one, just to give her a taste of what might be.

She looked up at him, surprised. She stayed very still, his arms around her, uncertain of what she should do. This is what sophisticated people do, she thought, when he kissed her lightly again.

'Dear, kind Claire,' he said, 'to be so forgiving when I did behave so badly.'

'No, really. It was my fault.'

He smiled down at her, his eyes close to hers. 'All right,' he said, 'we'll say it was all your fault. Oh, wicked Claire, to throw bread rolls at me.'

She began to laugh. 'And the glasses,' she exclaimed. 'And the way the butter went whoosh across the carpet.'

It was suddenly wonderful and they were both laughing and remembering, occasionally clutching at each other in their helpless mirth. The wine and the liqueur were coursing through her and she felt relaxed and not worried about anything, for wasn't everything suddenly right between them and she wasn't going to be sacked ever. The world out there, the world of everyday things, had disappeared like a hillside under cloud. Here it was real and there were different rules. She lay back, waiting for the next kiss.

His head hovered above hers.

'You look like a little bird in a nest, with its beak open,' he said, 'waiting.'

She felt caught out, wanted to deny it, but he was kissing her so she couldn't reply and soon didn't want to anyway.

He lifted her on to his knee, that being much the best position, in his experience, for a man to get his right hand inside a girl's blouse and his left hand up her skirt.

He held her like this for a long time, scarcely moving either hand at first, waiting until she reacted to the pressure. It was years since he had explored an unfamiliar body, discovered its preferences. He had forgotten the seductive delight of it.

'You'd be much comfier in bed,' he whispered to her at last.

Her body didn't deny it. He carried her, his hands still in the right places, across to the bedroom, where a single bedside lamp glowed. He didn't attempt to undress her, just held her very close until the moment came when she herself wanted everything off, and eagerly assisted in the process.

He nearly forgot himself, nearly forgot he was to be an observer in this game. It was such a long time since he had lain with such voluptuousness. She was full-breasted, tiny-waisted, wide-hipped. Oh, lovely, unfashionable shape, a wonderful change from slender elegance. To hell with slender elegance, he thought. A man needs these contrasts, he heard a voice saying. Whose voice? Ah, the MP for Flaxton West that night, that night she'd laughed at him.

He looked down at the body, the trusting body of a woman, how soft it is, how vulnerable. Not much mocking now. Yet above this woman's body the face was childish still, with its mass of hair spread across the pillows, what a golden halo it was. His hands left her body to play with her hair. Quickly, she snatched them back and replaced them where they had been before. Colin smiled to himself.

This is power, he thought, as he moved confidently about her. Like power over an audience, which is also a very enjoyable thing, it is about timing and response. Simple, like all power. Get her on your side, get her to do your will, let her show you what she wants, so that her will is the same as your will. Like this and like this and like this. Of course, it's calculating, but why not, if that's what she wants? Behold this Claire of mine, how pressing she is, how urgent, how eager. Soon the little cries will start, the imploring glances, the groans. But I shall not be lost with her. No, I shall be watching. This time I shall be doing all the smiling, because this time I am entirely in control.

117

Chapter Eighteen

'She seems much happier now, Claire, I mean,' Chrissie remarked, climbing into bed. 'More settled somehow, and she really loves her job. But what hours she works! I suppose it's all those late night sittings that MPs have, that keep her.'

Chrissie was vague about the ways of the House of Commons, and Claire had said little to enlighten her.

'Yes, they work crazy hours,' Jack agreed. 'But I must say she looks well on it. So I shouldn't worry, Chrissie. She's young enough to take it.'

'Oh, I'm not worried,' she assured him. 'And they're very good to her. They always send her home in a taxi.'

Her psyche had adjusted well, Claire reflected with satisfaction. The first few days had been understandably confusing and difficult. She had felt panic that he might have noticed the traces of blood and guessed the shameful secret of her virginity. But he had observed nothing and, as the days passed, her confidence grew.

The others in the office noticed the change in her. She always wore her hair in the French pleat now and it made her look older. Her face had lost that naive look, that rather jumpy expression that had made people fear she might do or say something unpredictable. She seemed to have grown up somehow. She had become discreet.

Claire knew she had found her role. This was the role that had always been there, somewhere in the muddle of her secret dreams. She did not see herself as an MP's compliant secretary, nor even as Emma Bovary, but as Madame de Pompadour, the power behind the throne. For Colin was a rising star and she was the great man's mistress. What a romantic role it was; sometimes she could hardly believe that it was hers. Perhaps she could not have believed it without his constant reassurance.

119

For what had started for Colin merely as a need to expiate the disaster of the dinner trolley, had swiftly moved into a passionate affair. It completed his life. When he murmured, 'You're so good for me, Claire,' as she lay in his arms, he spoke truly. He, Colin, had broken away from the bourgeois conventions of his youth. He moved among powerful men now, and powerful men had mistresses. He had become One of Us.

He often thought how lucky he was to live in the Eighties, a decade in which all the old moralities had been dumped. Only the impotent were faithful to their wives nowadays. That was the view of the business men among whom he increasingly mixed and who were accustomed to perks. A mistress was one of the perquisites of power.

Appetite grew with what it fed on. At every opportunity he summoned Claire to his flat, always with the excuse of work, for he observed the conventions for her sake. Sometimes, though rarely, he managed to arrange things so that she came there in the morning, when he happened, just happened, to be free.

Strangely, he and Betty were happier than ever. Perhaps not so strangely, he reflected, because a contented, satisfied husband can, of course, contribute better to his wife's happiness than a frustrated and lonely one. They had wonderful weekends. At garden parties in the constituency people smiled indulgently as they saw their MP and his wife holding hands, wandering from stall to stall. In the winter, at fund-raising dances, they made a handsome couple, glancing affectionately at each other across the hall, while dancing dutifully with as many of the party faithful as possible.

Chapter Nineteen

'I'll never forgive her, never,' Mrs Rawley said. 'Interfering little trouble-maker.'

'No, Janet, I've only myself to blame.'

'No, Geoff, you were persuaded.'

'I did wrong to let myself be.'

'And I went along with it.'

It was three years – it seemed a lifetime – since she'd come round, Claire had, and talked to them and given them the name of that man, that officer from the government, to go and see. Just under three years since they had sat in this very room, furnished and full of all their bits and pieces, and drunk sherry and Geoff had made a speech and kept looking at her and saying, 'Our own house, our very own.'

They'd had one bit of trouble almost straight away: bother with the chimney after a storm. Geoff had paid for insurance, though, so thought it would be all right but it seemed that the insurance didn't cover the first fifty pounds which was exactly what hiring the ladder and buying materials cost, plus a man to give him a hand for half a day. The fifty pound excess rule was to stop people claiming for small sums, they said. Well, fifty pounds might seem a small sum to some people but to Geoff it was getting on for half a week's wages.

It was all right, they managed, but it made them realise that the same words mean different things to different people when it comes to money.

Disaster struck nine months later in the form of rusting rods in the concrete of the walls, not just in their house but in plenty of others. But the difference was that the council still owned the others and paid for them to be put right. They'd have to pay for their own.

'That's all right,' Geoff had said. 'We've got the insurance. This is just the kind of thing you have insurance for.'

121

But it turned out to be not the kind of thing you have insurance for. Substandard construction, the insurance man told Geoff, was not an insured peril. This he translated to mean that they were not covered for it and would have to pay for the work themselves.

'He says what we ought to do,' Geoff told Janet afterwards, 'is to take out a second mortgage, you know, with a private company like a building society or a bank.'

'But we can't afford that,' she'd said, horrified.

'We can't afford not to,' he told her. 'The way I look at it is that we own a valuable asset in this house and it must be looked after, so it's worth taking out this extra loan to maintain its value.'

It frightened her, the way he was beginning to talk like one of them. But the work was carried out and they managed the mortgage payments as well as repaying the council, so all seemed well. Until. Until for some reason, understood by the other tribe, but not by Geoff, the mortgage rate went soaring up. What they had to repay each month almost doubled. They scraped along as best they could, saving on food and clothes. They had the telephone taken out – and were made to pay for that too. They sold their wedding presents, which didn't fetch much. They borrowed a bit from Janet's mother. And still they fell behind with their payments.

Finally the evening came when Janet said, 'Should we ask Mum again?' and Geoff said, 'No, it's the end of the road.'

He was holding in his hand the notice to quit.

It had come that morning and he hadn't been able to bring himself to show it to her.

'I'll go and see the council,' he said. 'It all started with them after all.'

But it didn't, she thought, it all started with that Claire.

The officer, who had organised their sale, had gone back to London, his work completed. But Geoff did see someone from the council, a Mr Robinson, a kindly man. A very sympathetic man. A powerless man.

'I'm very sorry, Mr Rawley,' he said. 'There are many others in your situation – which I know isn't any consolation.'

'But I can't understand it. They were all over us to buy and now nobody wants to know.'

'I'll be straight with you, Mr Rawley. We never wanted to sell off these houses. We knew they were needed; even then we had a waiting list. But we were forced; we were threatened with prosecution if we didn't sell off our housing stock.'

'Nobody warned us—'

'We wanted to prepare a document pointing out all the snags, but we weren't allowed to.'

'We just want to go back to things as they were,' Geoff pleaded desperately. 'We can pay the rent like we always did. We never fell behind in the old days.'

Mr Robinson shook his head. 'I'm sorry,' he said. 'Even if we let you fall behind with payments, your mortgage company won't. They have the right to reclaim their money from the sale of the house. They have the law on their side. It's very hard on you, but I'm afraid you'll have to leave.'

'But this money you've got from selling the houses, you'll have used that to build more houses, so surely we can go on the waiting list for one of them?'

Again the shaking of the head, again the apology. 'We're not allowed to use the money to rebuild, Mr Rawley.'

'You're telling me you've got the money and you can't build?' Geoff demanded, desperation giving way to anger. 'When there's any number of unemployed in the building trade? There's a brickie and two carpenters out of work in our street alone and a really good plasterer down the back, been unemployed for nearly two years.'

Mr Robinson sighed, he looked at his watch. He'd heard all this before.

'I'm afraid I can't offer you a council house, Mr Rawley,' he said. 'But although we have been forced to sell our houses and are not allowed to rebuild, we do still have a statutory obligation to house you. I suppose you might say we have responsibility without power.'

'But where does that leave *us*?' Geoff interrupted, not understanding what this man was on about.

'It means that we can arrange for you and your family to go into bed and breakfast accommodation. I can give you a list of places.'

She hadn't been able to believe it at first, Janet hadn't. She just couldn't take it in. It didn't make sense to force them out of their home where they'd lived all these years and make them go and live in one of those bed and breakfast places. Senseless or not, it happened.

123

She had never seen Geoff cry before, but he sat now in the empty front room of the home they were leaving, sat on an upturned tea-chest and wept with despair and shame. She went across to him, her steps loud and hollow on the bare boards, put her arms around him. The sound of his crying was horrible, a dry, rending sound like ripping up rags for cleaning.

'I've let you down,' he kept repeating between sobs. 'I've let you all down, you and the kids. Homeless! Us! Who've always managed. Homeless.'

It was a dreadful word, a death knell of a word.

'It's not you that's let us down,' she said fiercely. 'It's them with their lies and false promises.'

He didn't cry again and nor did she, not even in that bed and breakfast place where they couldn't sit round the table and talk as they used to, where there was nowhere for the children to do their homework in peace and quiet. Nowhere to cook. Nowhere to do the washing.

The kids soon got tired of trailing around, the four of them, looking for cheap places to eat, and began to wander off with their own friends. Some of them weren't very suitable either, especially Brian's. They just weren't the sort he used to bring home with him in the old days. Half the time she didn't know where he'd gone off to. She couldn't blame him; wouldn't any teenager go mad hanging about in a bedsitter with his family, no proper room of his own, no garage to go and make things, the way he used to? She dared not think what would happen when he left school next year. Homeless and jobless, what would he become? Other lads had drifted into petty crime. She had seen it.

But still she would not weep; she would not give them that satisfaction. Besides, grief soon gave way to anger, but being Mrs Rawley, it was an anger controlled, suppressed. So she went about her work dry-eyed, hard-faced, with bitterness in her heart. She would not allow self-pity, nor any other kind of pity, come to that.

Chapter Twenty

The encounters Colin enjoyed least were his Saturday morning surgeries. He had begun by having one every week but quickly cut it down to one a fortnight. They irritated him, most of the people who came to these surgeries, and this particular Saturday they seemed especially critical, none of them ardent party supporters, so it was hard to maintain a dutiful air of concern. He drove home thankful that the rest of the day was free for once.

It was only when he saw their car in the drive that he remembered about the visitors. Betty had told him that morning, but he'd forgotten. Her friend Kate and her husband, with Nell, were passing en route for somewhere or other and she had invited them in for lunch.

'We'll just have it in the morning room,' she had said. 'It's cosier.'

He had smiled as he kissed her and set off for the surgery. Such a sentence still had the power to delight one who had been brought up in a house whose downstairs rooms had consisted of a kitchen and a parlour.

She handed him a drink now as he came in to join them and he greeted them with all his easy charm; Betty's friend Kate, beautiful but dressed like a rag bag, her husband Luke, worthy but boring, and Nell who must be every bit of fifty, but still a handsome woman with those flecked brown eyes, luminously intelligent in the sculpted face. He didn't like her. Clever women were all right if they were clever in the way that Betty was clever, but Nell's cleverness was sharp, critical, uncompromising.

'How was surgery?' Betty asked him, as they sat down for lunch.

'Oh, the usual grumbles. The wrinklies are still complaining because they have to pay ten pounds for eye tests.'

125

'Well, they have had them free for forty years,' Betty pointed out.

'But really, all this fuss about ten pounds! What can you get for a tenner nowadays? You can't fill up the car for a tenner. You can't get a bottle of whisky for a tenner.'

'A third of your wrinklies don't have a car and most of them never drink whisky,' Luke pointed out.

'More to the point,' Nell said, 'if you're living on fifty pounds a week, ten pounds is a fifth of your income. The equivalent, for a wealthy man, would be about two hundred pounds, which you'd probably consider quite steep for an eye test.'

Oh, God, he'd forgotten she was an economist.

'It's not my department,' he said. 'Let me fill your glass.'

He's certainly handsome, Kate thought, watching him. Calculating, almost saturnine; she could imagine the ladies of the constituency responding to his call. But he lacked substance. What did he believe in? Power. Clearly he wanted power, but what was it for? Was it sufficient just to exercise it? Enjoy it, for its own sake, like sex? But no, how boring it must be, all those committee meetings, worthwhile and endurable only if you had a goal, pointless otherwise. But then, she reflected, no doubt her own activity would seem pointless to him, those boring hours of fruitless writing just because sometimes an idea came unbidden, a character came alive and took over its own destiny. But did it make up for those hours of non-achievement, for the guilt of knowing that, somewhere out there, neglected characters were hanging about with nowhere to go in their barren landscape?

Betty was laughing, offering potatoes evidently not for the first time. 'You still do it, Kate,' she said.

'What?'

'Go off in a dream.'

'I'm sorry.'

She helped herself to the potatoes, tiny new ones, buttery and garnished with finely chopped parsley.

'I don't know how you do it, Betty,' she said. 'You're so well organised. I mean, we're having this marvellous meal and you've hardly got up once. I'd have been shuttling between here and the kitchen, disappearing from the table for hours while I tried to resuscitate the latest calamity in the kitchen. And I've rows of parsley in the garden, but I'd never have got round to chopping it up for a garnish.'

'Do it all ahead, that's the secret.'

'Then the hot things go cold on me and the sauce turns to glue.'

They all laughed and Betty said, 'Ah, but you organise your novels and that's much more difficult.'

It was kindly meant but Kate wished the words unsaid. They would inevitably be followed by the And-what-are-you-working-on-now line of questioning. Luke jumped in, as she should have realised that he would, her protector and deflector.

'You're having a sabbatical term, aren't you, Nell?' he remarked. 'Are you doing something special with it?'

Bless him.

'Yes, I'm leading a team investigating the causes of homelessness,' Nell told him. 'The overall picture is of a very steep rise since the early Eighties. We have various subgroups, one looking into the lack of affordable rented accommodation, another into the impact of the sale of council houses, another into the effect of the rise in mortgage interest rates and the consequent dispossessions. I'm the one who tries to coordinate all their findings.'

'In my view,' Colin said, 'some people simply prefer to sleep rough and there's not much any government can do about it.'

'It's rather odd, isn't it, that this preference for homelessness only began to manifest itself in nineteen-eighty?'

Kate laughed. She couldn't help it. Good old Nell.

Colin controlled his annoyance.

'It has always been part of the human condition,' he said. 'There were tramps before the war.'

An intelligent man, Kate thought, couldn't have used such an argument. This man of Betty's was typical of modern politicians, shrewd and cunning, but somehow stupid. No wonder they so easily accepted their leader's shallow certainties.

'Will Sammy resign now that the press has got on to him?' Betty was asking.

For a moment none of the guests could think who Sammy was, and then realised that it was the pet name of one of Colin's colleagues, pictures of whom, with his actress girlfriend and loyal if exasperated wife, had bedecked the front pages of this morning's papers.

Colin nodded.

'It's disgraceful,' he said.

He looked around the table at his guests.

'Something will have to be done,' he pronounced, in the manner of a minister being interviewed on television. 'Something must be done about the press. Otherwise men of high ability are going to think twice before accepting public office, if they know that their private lives will be subject to such scrutiny.'

'Wouldn't it be simpler if they thought twice before having an affair?' Luke asked.

Kate knew that his question was genuine, but Colin didn't. Clearly he felt he was being got at.

'They order these things better in France,' he said irritably. 'Nobody cares if *their* ministers have mistresses.'

'Except their wives, presumably,' Betty remarked. 'And anyway, aren't you usually against the French way of doing things?'

But she smiled at him as she spoke because she liked the loyal way he was standing up for Sammy. Loyalty mattered a lot to Betty.

'If we're going to start imitating the French,' Luke said, 'I'd rather we copied their railway system than the supposed morality of their politicians.'

Colin dismissed the idea with a shrug and, getting up from the table, said, 'Shall we have coffee in here, darling?'

'Colin always makes the coffee,' Betty explained. 'He has one of those bubbly things.'

'It's my only domestic skill,' Colin told them, in the voice of one who was brought up far away from kitchens.

He moved over to the side table and busied himself with coffee beans and boiling water, meths and matches, and hoped they'd all soon go.

Later, in the huge master bedroom, Kate managed a quiet word with Betty before she left.

'How are things really?' she asked her friend.

Betty's face, so lively during lunch, was sad now in repose.

'Oh, it drags on,' she said wearily. 'They can't find any reason so far . . .'

Suddenly her eyes filled with tears. She took her friend's hand in hers.

'Just a baby, that's all I want,' she whispered, her voice breaking, 'but it seems it's too much to ask.'

Kate put her arms around her, knowing better than to burden her with consolations. Then after a while, she said, 'Shall we have a day together sometime? Just the two of us. In London, maybe? Galleries? Theatre? Lots of coffee and chat?'

'Oh, I'd love that. I've so many acquaintances here, you know, all of them conscious that I'm their MP's wife and it's the same in London, if I'm up there with Colin. I don't know why, but I don't seem to have any real friends any more. You're the only one I've talked to about this, Kate.'

'I know, I know.'

'I'm not being critical of Colin. He's very supportive. As I tell him, with the party always going on about family values, he's really obliged to produce one, isn't he?'

She managed a laugh, then, 'We'd better go down now. The others will be wondering. Shall I leave you to arrange it?'

'Yes. I'll be in touch. I'm better at organising theatres than dinner parties,' she added, as they went downstairs.

Chapter Twenty-one

It was going to be a warm day in London, but the early morning was chill and damp. Mist hung in the air and worked its way down escalators and along corridors and on to litter-strewn station platforms. Men who were sleeping rough in underground stations began to stir.

At Oxford Circus what appeared to be a bundle of rags turned and exposed a wizened face, brown-toothed and sunken-cheeked, to the world, which went unconcernedly by. Near it another bundle unleashed a thin and stick-like arm to grope for a bottle which, when it was found, was fumblingly uncorked by a trembling claw of a hand and raised to a toothless mouth below eyes which were red-rimmed, milky-blue and sightless.

In the archways of Westminster underground station, men were rolling up their blankets and storing away their cardboard boxes. The smell of urine and stale breath permeated the air. While above, in the arched corridors of Westminster, only a pavement away, the lawmakers who had ordained this underworld would soon be going unwittingly about their business.

At Victoria station Betty was approached by a woman she had never seen before and so, for a moment, took to be one of Colin's constituents.

'Please,' the woman said, 'can you spare me a little money? I'm not used to begging, truly I'm not, but I can't get the social security until I've got an address and I'm homeless.'

Betty gave her money and walked on, trembling. Beggars in London? She had never in her whole life seen a beggar in England. Beggars were people in India or Southern Italy, but here? A few years ago it would have been unthinkable. Whatever was happening to England?

She was out of touch, she told herself, as she walked across to the underground. She'd read about the beggars, of course, but it was a different matter to see one, a woman like herself, face to face. She was still thinking about it when her train came in.

A man was standing by the door, although there were plenty of empty seats. As the train moved off he began haranguing the passengers, waving his arms and shouting. They sat, embarrassed by his madness, unwilling to be involved. Men hid their faces behind newspapers, women gave him pitying glances, but quickly looked away again, not wanting to catch his eye.

She was glad to change trains, leaving somebody else to cope. But what on earth was he doing here, on the underground? The next train was almost empty, the rush hour over, just herself and one other woman in the compartment, until another woman jumped in. At first she wasn't sure if it was a woman. Ageless, sexless, she was dressed in a kind of sack, with a cord around her middle and a pair of galoshes made out of cut-down wellington boots on her feet. Her face was ingrained with dirt and her grey hair was a wiry tangle. Mrs John the Baptist, Betty thought irreverently.

Then the woman began to rant. She raged at the empty compartment. She took off her shoes and untied the cord around her waist. For the rest of the journey Betty sat, outwardly cool and composed in her pale beige linen suit, but inwardly terrified that the woman would remove the sack, and dreading the sight of the shrunken body beneath.

Kate was waiting for her, as arranged, at Paddington Station. She was looking fit and well, Betty observed, as if she'd spent the summer in the garden. She was wearing a loose blue garment of indeterminate age and shape and flat shoes, but she was so pretty with her glowing skin and curly dark hair that somehow one didn't notice the disaster area underneath. Or rather, one did but it didn't seem to matter.

'Oh, it's lovely to see you, Kate,' she said. 'And I've had such a ghastly time crossing London.'

She told her about the two deranged people on the underground. Kate didn't seem particularly surprised.

'It's called Community Care,' she said.

Betty looked at her, baffled.

'But you're often in London,' Kate said. 'You must have seen them before.'

'I don't often go on the underground,' Betty admitted. 'I only did today because you sent me all the instructions.'

'They're getting rid of psychiatric beds,' Kate said. 'Sending the patients out. A lot of them have nowhere to go and drift on to the underground. It's warm, I suppose, and feels safe.'

'But they were so pathetic, especially the woman. And I dread to think what might happen to the poor thing if she was surrounded by the wrong sort of people. Drunken men, you know the sort of thing.'

'Why don't you ask Colin? He's in a position to do something about it, after all.'

Betty hesitated. 'He says Members of Parliament have much less power than people think.'

'Maybe, but it's still a lot more than the rest of us have,' Kate said brusquely. She suspected that the real reason was that he didn't care and Betty knew it.

'Look,' she said, pointing to the row of bags on the bench beside her, 'I've brought you some windfalls. And these are the last of the new potatoes, which I've just dug up. They're delicious and they'll keep all right – I've left plenty of soil on them. And here are a few pears. They're going sleepy so eat them up quickly. They're fine for stewing anyway. And here are a couple of marrows and some courgettes. Oh, and a few baby carrots, late sowings, you know.'

Betty gazed at the assorted packages in dismay.

'I know your grounds are vast and so beautiful,' Kate was saying, 'but not very productive, are they? Mostly ornamental.'

'But we can't carry that lot around London,' Betty protested.

'Oh, I don't mind. I'm used to humping garden produce about. It's no trouble.'

'I suppose we could leave it in the left luggage office?'

'No, it's closed for security reasons.'

'Then let's take it all round to the flat and drop it off there. Colin can bring it up on Friday. He has to take part in a debate at the university before he comes home, so your vegetables are going to be well travelled before we eat them. I'd like to show you the flat anyway and we can have some coffee while we're there. I need it.'

Kate took a diary out of her bag and began studying a map of the underground in the front.

'Oh, stuff that,' Betty said. 'I've had enough of the underground for one day. We're going by taxi.'

In the cab, with all the vegetables and fruit ranged at their feet, she suddenly burst out laughing.

'Honestly it looks like a harvest festival in here. It's really sweet of you,' she added impulsively, taking Kate's hands in her own. They both looked down at them, the white ones, with their immaculate pink nails, and the workworn brown ones with traces of what looked like compost round the cuticles.

'It's the stain from nipping out the side shoots on the tomatoes,' Kate explained. 'I ought to wear gloves.'

'Now or when you nip out the side shoots?'

'Both.'

Betty laughed. 'Don't change, Kate,' she said. 'Don't ever change.' Then more seriously, she went on, 'If you can bear it, I'd like to tell you all about this baby thing when we have coffee in the flat.'

'If you think it will help.'

'Yes, I think it will. My bloody brothers are multiplying like rabbits, of course. I can't talk to Mother, never have been able to. Colin's okay about it, but really he has so much on his mind with the constituency, he can do without the distraction, and you know the social life is pretty hectic and – oh, here we are.'

They shared the bags of garden produce between them as they climbed out of the taxi. It was a beautiful morning, sunny but with the crispness of autumn edging the air.

'It's only a tiny flat,' Betty said, as she unlocked the door. 'But very handy for Colin and surprisingly quiet for London. It really is quite peaceful with that little square opposite.'

'The lime trees could do with pollarding,' Kate remarked, briefly looking back at the square, before following Betty into the flat.

The sitting room, she noticed, was quite large despite what Betty had said. There was a bedroom beyond; the door into it was open. She saw that somebody was in Betty's bed; a man and a woman. They looked up and she saw that it was Colin. For a moment she did not recognise the woman, just had a hazy impression of a red face, a pair of large breasts, flushed pink, and a great deal of fair, rather fuzzy hair. Then she recognised Chrissie's daughter.

Nobody moved; the whole scene seemed frozen. They were figures in a tableau. Then Kate moved protectively forward in front of her friend. But Betty stepped into the bedroom. She was very pale. She looked long and hard at the bed, as if determined to memorise every detail. Then, 'Come on, Kate,' she said. 'We don't want to be late for the matinée.'

Chapter Twenty-two

'Could you turn out the room below the stairs today, Mrs Rawley?' Chrissie asked. 'I'm afraid it's in a dreadful mess.'

'There'd be no point in doing it if it was clean and tidy,' Mrs Rawley told her, taking off the grey jacket and donning the brown overall.

'That's true, but the dust will make you thirsty, so do help yourself to plenty of coffee.'

Mrs Rawley, busy gathering together buckets and cloths, didn't reply.

Chrissie worried about her. She didn't really need her help now that Rosemary was growing up and going to full-time school, but she knew Mrs Rawley needed the money, so made extra jobs for her to do. Not that Mrs Rawley ever spoke of her troubles; she was far too reserved for that. What really worried Chrissie was the change that had come over her in the last year. She had never looked exactly cheerful, but always calm. Now calmness had hardened. There was an implacable expression on her face, a bitterness about the mouth. Her eyes looked warily at the world, suspicious and watchful for further hurt. It made her an uneasy person to be with.

Kate, who had seen her once or twice recently, had called her the Madame Defarge of Barrow Court and asked if she brought her knitting with her. It was all cleverness to Chrissie but, when Kate explained, she could see what she meant: there was something a bit sinister about Mrs Rawley's suppressed rage.

She remembered that conversation as she laid out the coffee things and put Mrs Rawley's wages beside them.

'I'm off now,' she called in the direction of the stairs. 'See you tomorrow morning.'

It wasn't your usual cupboard under the stairs, big enough to hold the hoover and a few brushes. It was a huge place; you

135

went down two steps to it. It was a cross between a cellar and a garden shed, Mrs Rawley thought, as she began lifting down vases and bulb bowls, old tennis rackets and hockey sticks, boxes of electrical bits and pieces and stuff for flower arranging. All the sort of things they'd really no use for, but didn't want to throw out. Put it into limbo under the stairs. Then there were all these preserving jars; nobody used them nowadays, not with freezers they didn't. Nobody had looked at them since she dusted them last year, she reckoned, as she began wiping the shelves with a damp cloth. A bit of a hoarder, Chrissie was. She should get rid of them.

Just thinking the words sent an unexpected jab of pain through her as she suddenly remembered all the things she herself had had to get rid of. They'd stored some of the furniture at her mum's, some with various members of Geoff's family, but, once scattered, would it ever be reassembled? Some things, once broken, can't be mended. Like homes, like trust.

If only Geoff had listened more to her and less to that officer from London, not that she'd ever say so, because he'd acted for the best. But she'd told him over and over again that a home is a home, rented or bought, and secure it must be. The other tribe might think a home was an investment; they'd never thought like that, she and Geoff. A home was a home, nothing more and nothing less and nothing other.

She stopped suddenly and listened. Someone was coming in the front door. She was surprised; they were out at work, all of them. Nobody was expected back or Chrissie would have said. Well, it didn't sound like an intruder, she thought, as she put the cloth back in the bucket and prepared to go and investigate. They were making far too much noise for that.

They were charging upstairs now, whoever they were; ah, it must be Claire, that was her bedroom door that had just slammed. She shrugged slightly; it didn't sound as if she was ill, so best leave it alone, she thought, as she went on wiping down the shelves. More likely some row at work. She rubbed the shelves with a dry cloth and began replacing the preserving jars which nobody would touch until she dusted them again next year.

The telephone rang in the hall. She was moving things out of the way so she could get through to answer it, when Madam came tearing downstairs, making even more noise than when she went up. Let her answer it.

'Oh, I'm so glad you've rung, darling. Oh, whatever shall we do?'

So that was it: man trouble.

A lot of exclaiming and occasional weeping and wailing was going on out there. Making a drama of it, Madam was. Well, it wasn't her business. Mrs Rawley tried not to listen to any of it, but couldn't help hearing, not with just one bit of floor boarding between her head and the telephone.

'You really think it can be kept quiet . . . try to explain . . . can't you see her tonight . . . no, of course, Colin, I'm sorry . . . no, of course not, she won't want her name in the papers any more than you do . . . oh, thank you, darling, for ringing . . . so comforting . . . always . . . no, I do understand . . . bless you . . . Yes, I know . . . me too . . .'

Evidently she stood for a while by the phone, Madam did, because there was no sound of movement. Then Mrs Rawley heard her mutter something which sounded like, Please God, Let Me Get Away With It, or words to that effect. Then she heard footsteps going slowly, heavily upstairs and the sound of Claire's bedroom door shutting more quietly this time.

Mrs Rawley was not, by nature, a vengeful woman. She had never had cause to be. Her mistakes had been her own responsibility and she had never blamed anybody else for them. Her life might have been narrow but she had been in control of it – until three years ago. Then outside forces had smashed into her life, taken away her home, broken up her family, put her children at risk, hurt her nearest and dearest, shamed and humiliated them all. She didn't understand these forces so she didn't blame the bigotry of politicians. Instead she personalised these evil forces so that they took on the shape of the one who had persuaded them to take the first step towards buying their house: her employer's daughter.

'I'll never forgive her' was the phrase she often used, as for the first time in her life she felt a thirst for vengeance. Now, among the tennis rackets and preserving jars, she had been given the means of slaking it.

She finished her work, left everything in order. She picked up her wages from the kitchen table, but somehow couldn't bring herself to drink the coffee that had been left out for her. For something gave her pause: compassion for Chrissie. After all, Claire was Chrissie's daughter. Then bitterness plucked at her lips as she reflected that she too had a daughter, a daughter who had once had a bedroom of her own with all her treasures in it, a garden to play in, a home which her friends could visit and be made welcome. No pity had been shown to her, just a notice to quit. Injustice had to be avenged.

She didn't stop to think, as she put on her grey jacket and prepared to leave the house, that the same forces which had made her vengeful and bitter had helped Claire along the road of selfishness and greed. Her decision was taken even before she let herself out of the house.

The next decision was a relatively minor one: to which newspaper she should take her story.

Chapter Twenty-three

Chrissie was worried about Claire. Though for once she had come home early yesterday, she had stayed in her bedroom, curtains drawn, and refused her supper, even when offered something on a tray. When her mother tried to comfort her, she had turned away. She had obviously been crying and seemed frightened.

'Is something wrong at work, darling?' Chrissie had asked. Her only reply had been an even more frightened look in those dark eyes and a request to be left in peace to go to sleep.

She had looked in at her before leaving for work, but Claire was lying in the dark, not stirring, so she just shut the door quietly and left her to sleep on. Maybe it was just all these late nights catching up with her, Chrissie told herself. She wanted to believe that, but instinct told her that something more than overwork was wrong with her daughter.

She tried to put it out of her mind as she went into the hospital, for she had trained herself, ever since she started nursing, not to take her everyday concerns into the hospital with her; worries had to be left, like dirty laundry, outside the ward. Just as a teacher must be bright and cheerful with the children in the classroom, even if her own child is sick or her parents dying, so it seemed to Chrissie that a nurse must always be serene on duty whatever anxieties troubled her mind at home.

So into this different world she went, doing all the routine things, checking notes with the outgoing staff, giving medicines, consoling Mrs Plaister, a retired headmistress who had just had a second eye operation and was old and frail and anxious.

'Couldn't I just stay in for one more day, Sister?' she was begging. 'I do feel very shaky still. When I had the other eye done, I was in a week.'

'I'm sorry, Mrs Plaister,' she had to say, 'but you're due to leave this morning, so we'll get you up now. You can sit here in a comfortable chair while you wait. A taxi is coming for you, isn't it?'

'Oh, yes, it's all arranged. But I was just hoping that I might stay another night until I feel a bit stronger. I don't want to be a bother of course but—'

'I'll have a word with the doctor,' Chrissie interrupted, unable to bear the sight of this dignified old lady reduced to begging so pitifully, 'and see what we can do.'

She was on duty with Faith McBain, a caustic Scot nearing retirement, who had worked in the National Health Service all her life. Chrissie decided to talk to her first.

'I don't think she's fit to go out, Faith.'

'Of course she isn't. Could do with another three days.'

'She says she was in a week when her other eye was done. Have the procedures changed much since then, do you think?'

'No, but the system has. They've cut the number of beds and you know what our bed manager's like.'

Oh yes, she knew what Mr Pickton, the bed manager, was like.

'Could you speak to him, Faith? I know it's up to the doctor to decide but Mr Pickton does seem to have a lot of influence.'

'Scared of the old Pickaxe, are you?'

'I just think he'd pay more attention to you if you explained about the health of the patient. You've more experience than I have.'

Faith McBain looked at her severely.

'Try to understand, Chrissie, that what matters to him is not the state of the patient, but the state of the statistics.'

Suddenly she relented. 'Don't look so crestfallen, Chrissie, I'll see what I can do.'

In the event, Mr Pickton came into the ward while Faith was away transferring another patient. The doctor hadn't been available; Mrs Plaister had already been taken down to her taxi.

Godfrey Pickton was a tall, thin man whose head seemed too small for the rest of him. He had a sharp, pointed little face and his features seemed to converge at the tip of his nose, as if someone had put their thumb under his chin and their fingers on his brow and squeezed hard.

He stood in the middle of the ward: four beds on one side, three on the other.

'Who can we get rid of?' he asked.

One by one he stared at them, those docile, helpless figures, as they lay in bed. He questioned her about each in turn. Chrissie kept her voice low but he did not. She knew that they all, except Miss Burchell who was very deaf, heard everything that he said, heard him asking which one of them could be got rid of. They watched him anxiously with baleful, frightened eyes.

'What about that one?'

'Mrs Peach? A colostomy patient. The operation went very well but Mr Dunlop is concerned about her breathing so he's asked Dr Clutterbuck to look at her tomorrow morning on his rounds.'

'I hope that was officially registered.'

Chrissie couldn't think of an adequate reply so said nothing.

Mr Pickton seemed distracted for a moment; he nodded his pointed little head up and down, his neck swaying slightly on his long body, like a praying mantis. Then he returned to the matter in hand.

'What about her?' he asked.

'Mrs Jackson? No, she hasn't recovered her balance yet. She will. She's made very good progress. Mr Dunlop is very pleased with her.'

'How old is she?'

'Seventy-one.'

'Then she could be sent to Fairview.'

'She's not senile,' Chrissie said, lowering her voice to a whisper.

'Maybe not, but she's over seventy.'

'But—'

'She's a bed blocker. Explain to her that we've given it considerable thought and feel sure she doesn't want to be malingering here in hospital. I'll make a few telephone calls and let you know the outcome.'

Without a backward glance, he strode out of the ward, prancing on his long legs in a way which had led some of the younger nurses to nickname him The Galloping Hairpin.

'I am not senile,' Mrs Jackson said sharply. 'Nor am I malingering. I just wish to stay here until I am better.'

Chrissie was going over to her bed when Mrs Plaister was brought back into the ward, having collapsed as she was getting into her taxi. Faith, coming in just in time, helped her get the old lady back into bed.

Godfrey Pickton came in as she was writing the report.

'Mrs Plaister collapsed, Mr Pickton,' she told him. 'She's back in bed now. The doctor has examined her and says she's just fainted from post-operative weakness. She'll be all right in a couple of days, but he'll check her again before she goes out.'

The bed manager clicked his tongue with disapproval.

'Is this really necessary?' he asked.

'Absolutely,' Faith said, coming into the room behind him. 'Unless you want another case like Mr Samson.'

Mr Samson had been sent home still bleeding after a prostatectomy. Two days later he was rushed in during the night and died an hour later. The case was complicated by the fact that his surgeon had said that he was to stay in longer but, while he was on holiday, Mr Pickton found another consultant prepared to declare that the old man was fit to go home.

'Very well,' he agreed reluctantly now. 'Had Mrs Plaister been discharged?' he asked suddenly.

'Yes.'

'Good.' His face brightened. 'That means that this counts as another admission.'

'But she never really left—'

'She was discharged and has now been readmitted,' Mr Picton insisted. 'She had left the building. Officially she had left our care,' he added, as he went out of the room.

'If indeed she was ever in it,' Faith McBain whispered to his retreating back. ' "We are mistreating more patients than ever before in our entire history",' she added, in a passable imitation of the saccharine tones of the Minister of Health.

Chrissie laughed despite herself.

'That's better,' Faith said. 'You haven't been looking quite your cheerful self today. Anything wrong?'

'I'm all right, thank you.'

'Just to add to your joys, the Nurse Manager wants to see you before you go off this evening.'

'Oh, no!'

Chrissie found the Nurse Manager intimidating; Francesca Brassington was one of those nurses recruited to join the management in an attempt to win the staff over to changes they had hitherto opposed. It suited her well; she enjoyed organising, was good with computers and had never liked the patients anyway. A tall, statuesque woman with blonde hair and aquiline features, she might well have been a model, Faith McBain had once suggested, for the ideal of Teutonic beauty so much admired in Nazi Germany. Her eyes, bright and penetrating, were as blue as sapphire, and as hard. In a more forgiving mood, Faith had once said, 'I bet she was always chosen to act Portia in the school play, though she'd have had a bit of trouble with the speech about mercy.'

'Did she say what she wanted to see me about?' Chrissie asked now.

'No. She wouldn't, would she? Keep people guessing, that's her management philosophy, keep them on their toes, insecurity is good for others. Unsettle everybody as much as you possibly can and as for the poor old patients – sorry, customers – if they call for a bedpan give them a charter.'

'There's one good piece of news,' Faith told her as they were going off duty. 'They spoke to Mrs Jackson's children and later had a call from a Mr Bugle. Mr Bugle is a hospital manager in Birmingham. He is also Mrs Jackson's son-in-law. So she'll not be dumped in Fairview. Poor old Pickaxe picked the wrong one this time,' she added, laughing.

Chrissie couldn't laugh with her. Somebody else, who didn't have a powerful son-in-law, would be targeted instead. Besides, now that work was over, anxiety about Claire could no longer be kept at bay.

A few minutes later she was in the Nurse Manager's office, formerly a waiting room for visitors of seriously ill patients.

'Come in and do sit down,' Francesca Brassington said, flashing Chrissie a professionally welcoming smile. Then she fixed her with her basilisk eyes and said, 'I believe you lent a chest drain to a medical ward last Monday?'

Chrissie remembered the emergency.

'Yes,' she said. 'I did.'

'And you failed to charge for it.'

'It was urgent. They needed it immediately for a patient.'

'Urgency is no excuse. The internal market requires that everything is correctly accounted for. Equipment is not borrowed in the casual way it once was. It has to be charged for. Please remember that in future.'

'Yes. I'm sorry.'

The Nurse Manager bestowed a brief and chilling smile of

forgiveness, before going on, 'Also, I've been looking through the reports and I think you are perhaps insufficiently aware of the system of referrals to consultants. If the consultant in charge of one of the people in your care requires them to see another consultant then this is classified as a separate consultant episode. It must be registered as such and the appropriate computer entries made. This is of vital importance, otherwise how can we measure our achievement?'

It seemed to Chrissie that there were other, more human, ways of measuring achievement, but she knew better than to say so.

'Also,' Francesca Brassington went on, 'I gather you expressed concern about the lack of beds for admissions?'

'Yes, it causes such stress. Particularly for women with young families. They have to make all the arrangements for their children to be looked after and then at the last minute we have to tell them there isn't a bed. It happened to one patient, a Mrs Barley. She was being prepared for theatre when we had an emergency and needed her bed, so had to send her home. She was nearly breaking down, she was so distressed about her family. I just don't think it should happen.'

'That's hardly for you to decide,' the cold voice pointed out, as the blue eyes stared at her, cold and hard as marbles. 'We are not, as the Minister so often points out, in the business of counting beds.'

But we are, Chrissie thought, we are. Hours of valuable time are spent trying to find beds. Wouldn't it be more sensible just to provide more of them? Or anyway stop reducing them. And more economical, since that's what they're always on about. But she knew that such a simple view of things would never find favour, so didn't argue.

She came out of the interview bewildered, not sure what it had all been about, except that she had been, in some obscure way, warned. Recently she had begun to think that perhaps people like Faith and herself no longer fitted into the new way of doing things. She knew that she had been preoccupied at home, worrying about work. It wasn't fair on the others, she thought, on Rosemary, Jack and especially on Claire, who seemed to be in some sort of trouble. Perhaps she would be better to give up nursing and limit her caring to her own family.

For caring was in her nature; it was what she needed to do.

She had wanted to nurse for as long as she could remember, but her parents had forbidden it when she left school. So she had achieved her life's ambition later than most, and though it had been a struggle doing all that studying when she was no longer young, she had loved every minute of it.

She could not have imagined, a few years ago, that she would ever feel like this, she thought, as she made her way to the bus stop. Recently she had heard other nurses say that they just wanted to get out, take early retirement, anything, but she had always told herself that what really mattered was looking after the patients and nothing and nobody could spoil that. But now she was beginning to feel that she couldn't do her job as it should be done, could not give the patients the reassurance they needed. She knew the pain of doing something she really cared about, and not being allowed to do it as it should be done.

So better, perhaps, not to do it at all, she thought. But then she remembered Mrs Plaister and old Miss Burchell and the others like them and knew that she couldn't desert them, whatever regimes were inflicted on her by the likes of Mr Pickton and Francesca Brassington. Somebody had to be there to defend people who were too frail to fight for themselves.

It had only seemed worse today because she was tired, she told herself as she sat on the bus, and had been worried about Claire. Probably when she got home Claire would be up and about and quite back to her normal, confident self. Hungry too, probably, Chrissie thought as she turned her mind to what she was giving her family for supper.

She was still planning the meal as she got off the bus and began the short walk home, so at first didn't notice anything unusual, except that there seemed to be more traffic about. She was nearly there before she realised that it was her own house that was surrounded with cars and reporters and photographers.

Chapter Twenty-four

He could have done without this wretched university debate, Colin reflected, as he drove to it. He had no doubt that he could sort things out with Betty; she was reasonable, she was worldly-wise, she would dismiss it for the peccadillo that it was. It had happened before and it would happen again, so long as there were men and women on this earth.

Thank God he'd chosen such a woman for his wife, tolerant and sensible. She was loyal too. He could depend on her to stand by him through thick and thin. He pitied his colleagues who had married lesser women. He despised them in a way for showing so little foresight, so little calculation, in their choice. Politicians should have better judgement.

He'd give up the girl, of course. That went without saying. It was the only honourable course. But he needed to sort it all out with Betty now, without delay. Delay would only complicate things, especially as tomorrow was the day of the great autumn fair, the biggest fund-raising event of his constituency party. He'd left her a message, saying he could explain everything and apologising for upsetting her. It must have been a shock for her, coming on them like that. It was a shock for him too – he shivered as he remembered it. Of course, if only she'd told him she was coming to the flat, none of this would have happened.

The debate wouldn't be a problem. The subject was, 'The Thatcher Miracle: Fact or Fiction?' He'd have no difficulty presenting the motion; he'd always got the tame statisticians to provide a sheaf of statistics to prove anything that it was necessary to prove. A professor was speaking against it, probably academic and not well versed in this kind of thing, used to lecturing students, not manipulating their minds. That was something politicians learned pretty quickly. Normally he'd have been looking forward to it.

But the times weren't normal and he should have been sorting

out Betty this evening. Ah, well at least there was no publicity.
Even if there were, his colleagues would rally round, men of the
world, all of them, but of course there was no fear of that. Claire
was a sensible lass. He'd find her another job. One of his many
business associates would be delighted to have her.

Nell picked up the telephone. 'Hello,' she said, vaguely, her mind
still on the paper she was writing. On the other end of the line, the
Dean, James Chester, sounded urgent.

'I'm on the scrounge, Nell. It's a great favour I'm asking, I know.
Well, not for myself, actually, but for Ned Taylor. He's supposed to
be leading the debate tonight – agreed months ago – and he's too
ill. He'd hoped to be over the worst, but it's out of the question,
a really virulent strain of flu and, apart from anything else, he's
no voice.'

'I can smell what's coming,' Nell said. 'How about doing it
yourself?'

'I can't, Nell, truly I can't. I'm hosting this dinner for the
Americans tonight. We're hoping for serious money. I can't drop
out now. I wish I could. I seem to spend most of my waking hours
nowadays going round with the begging bowl. It's not what I came
into this profession for – it used to be about teaching and research
in those days.'

'James,' she interrupted, 'you haven't told me what the debate's
about.'

'Oh, yes, I'm sorry. It's the one called "The Thatcher Miracle: Fact
or Fiction?" Ned was taking the fiction side.'

'Of course, yes, I've seen the notices.'

'An MP's on the other side. Colin Baker.'

'Oh, my God!'

'Know him?'

'Yes, not particularly well. He's married to a friend of my
cousin.'

'Ned says you can have his notes. They're all ready for you. I'll
have them sent up.'

The notes arrived with a bouquet of flowers, which she put
immediately into water. The notes she put in the wastepaper bin
a little while later.

He had been warned that student audiences can be difficult,

but Colin didn't find this one so. The welcome was polite, the preliminaries efficient. Seeing Nell was something of a surprise, but even that he could take in his stride. He told his audience how dire had been the state of Britain until the government which he was proud to support took over and wrought its miracle. He told them how much better off everyone was now, how taxation was lower and morale higher. He told them there was much still to be done, scroungers still to be rooted out, but greatness had indubitably been restored. The clichés rolled, the audience hearkened. He rounded it off by warning that equality was a myth, self-interest the only motive force. Trying to be fair never worked, he said, and told them that the attempt at rationing in the last war had failed and the black market flourished. Money is the only effective rationer of goods, he said. He sat down to polite applause; he would listen courteously to Nell while at the same time starting to compose his speech to his wife.

Nell had expected most of this and had her replies ready. What had surprised her, enraged her so much that she was taken aback even by her own anger, were his remarks about the war. She set aside her notes and, still enraged, waded in.

'I'm older than any of you here,' she began, 'including my opponent. I will therefore be charitable and put down to ignorance rather than unpatriotic malice his comments about the war and rationing. At a time when Britain was in mortal danger, a fair and honest system was worked out – incidentally, by a Conservative, Lord Woolton. Even I was too young to know about it at first hand, but I can tell you that when I went to France as a schoolchild after the war people spoke of it there with respect. They had not been able to have such a system, the black market prevailed in a way which would have been unthinkable here. "Ah, but in England you have Le Fair Play," I remember them saying again and again. And I remember feeling proud of being British, not in the chauvinistic way which is popular today, but with a quieter pride. I am sorry that you have been deprived of that kind of pride in the ways of your country. Jingoism is a poor substitute.'

The audience was attentive; Colin gazed at the ceiling.

'You have heard what he had to say about the Bad Old Days,' Nell went on. 'Some of us actually lived through them. It was the Bad Old Days which provided my opponent, like his leader, with a grant to go to university. He wasn't saddled with a loan, as

149

students soon will be if the government goes ahead with its plans. He didn't have to wait for weeks for money to come through or give up his place because it didn't come through in time, as has happened here. If that security was right for him, why should it be wrong for you? Or is he saying that it damaged him?

'I remember the Bad Old Days when dentistry was free, when councils were allowed – indeed were obliged – to provide good housing, when we had clean streets, better transport and towns without beggars. He says we can't afford these things now. Isn't it strange that we managed it in the Bad Old Days?

'I must tell you, who are too young to remember a different England, that there was a time when people didn't need to barricade themselves into their homes or walk fearfully in the streets, a time when governments thought of all the people, not just a section of them. Of course it was hard. There were no oil revenues in those days. Assets were being built up, not sold off. Factories, houses, stations had been destroyed by bombing, everything had to be repaired, rebuilt, and yet in all that devastation we could create a health service that was the admiration of the world. How did we do it in the Bad Old Days? It is simple; there was the political will.

'And why can't we do it now? Because that will has gone. How can we talk of shortage of money when we have had in this decade more than a hundred billion pounds in oil revenues alone? When we have sold assets for untold billions? Will future generations believe that the British public actually paid this government billions of pounds to buy what it already owned? And that the money vanished, so that all the benefits of the Bad Old Days were suddenly no longer affordable? So that even after this economic miracle, in which my opponent so fervently believes, we can't afford all those things which we managed to provide in those Bad Old Days?'

She sat down to a round of applause. Colin looked at his watch. It was all going on far too long. The questions surprised him too. He had underestimated this audience. They knew their facts. An American got up and asked why the government was always trying to imitate America. His country, he said, was more divided than ever before, the Have-Nots were resentful and the Haves scared. Colin fielded it as best he could by saying relationships between our Prime Minister and the American President had never been better. For some reason that evoked mirth.

It was the question which fired Nell's final peroration. 'We are busily creating,' she said, 'just such a society of Haves and Have-Nots. We are sowing the seeds. When the homeless, the unemployed and the unheeded fight back, not with open rebellion because that is not our way, but with crime and vandalism, we shall reap the harvest. Those to whom society gives nothing, owe it nothing in return. Not that the government will admit it, when the time comes. They will find scapegoats; they will blame everything from human nature to the weather. They will talk as if this is the one harvest in history which was never sown, as if they had never done anything – or failed to do anything – which brought it about.'

Colin was by now resigned to losing the motion. He hadn't expected to lose it quite so ignominiously. He was used to winning. For the first time he began to think that perhaps something was going wrong, something which might lose him his seat at the next election, that would deprive him of power and, worse still, of prestige. He might end up by being just a common man again; the thought appalled him as he left the hall. He dismissed such thoughts. Nell was a rabble-rouser, that was all. No, he wouldn't stay for a drink, thank you. He must be off. He had to deal with another lady who might prove troublesome: his wife.

Chapter Twenty-five

There was a mistiness in the air and a heavy dew on the grass as they began putting up the stalls for the annual fête. It promised to be a sunny, cloudless day. But if the weather was perfect, the atmosphere was not. Usually, on this day of days, the workers moved about briskly with smiles on their faces and confidence in their step as they put up tents, spread stalls with white sheets, opened tins full of sponge cakes and home-made biscuits and arranged jars of jam and chutney. Usually they joked as they put up the ropes for bowling for the pig, draped curtains over the pagoda in which Lucy Maggot told fortunes, tipped pounds of sawdust into that old favourite, the bran tub, or counted out hoops in fives for the hoop-la stall. Usually the women who laid out the cups and saucers in the big marquee did it with much gossiping as well as clattering of tin trays and later they all chatted as they counted out three sandwiches, a piece of cake and a biscuit on each plate.

Today the money-raising sociability was subdued. They moved about their tasks quietly, corners of mouths tucked anxiously in, exchanging few words, and those guardedly, with none of the confident affability of yesteryear. They had brought out old divisions too, these rumours had. Those who hadn't supported Colin's candidature in the first place, but who had forgotten their opposition in the days of his success, remembered it now. Those who had become friends of Betty, felt partisan rage; hadn't she slaved away down here for him, hadn't she given up her job, devoted time and energy to the constituency? Others murmured that infidelity was commonplace nowadays; even the future king was rumoured to be guilty of it. So if royalty could commit adultery, why shouldn't the MP for Boxley? But they knew better than to say it in the presence of their member's wife's fan club.

At least, they were all agreed, it was a good thing they hadn't moved the fête into the grounds of the Manor House, as Colin had suggested they might. Thank goodness, they had kept away from the matrimonial home. Here, in the field and paddock that belonged to the agent, they were, in every sense, on safer ground.

It all depended on Colin and Betty, everyone agreed on that too. If they arrived smiling, hand-in-hand, looking as if they had just weathered one of those domestic storms which arise, after all, in every marriage at some time or another, then they could all breathe a corporate sigh of relief and pretend it had never happened. In this hope, the party faithful went about their annual tasks, doggedly setting up stalls and arranging tombolas with little of their usual joy but at least comforted by the familiar routine of it all.

They arrived together. Betty was, they observed, perhaps just a little pale, though it was hard to tell under that lovely olive-green, wide-brimmed hat. She was elegant, as always, in a simple green and yellow linen dress. Fool of a chap, that Colin, some of the men thought, to cheat on such a peach of a girl; peccadillo, muttered others, each to his own preferred cliché.

'My wife,' Colin told his agent, 'has agreed to say a few words.'

'Oh, I'm so glad,' the agent said, taking her hand and shaking it warmly, then holding it in his own to show his utter support. The Boxley Conservative Association, his body language said, thanks you from the bottom of its corporate heart.

The green eyes looked back at him. She smiled.

They climbed, the three of them, on to a little dais which was decorated with as many blue flowers as the flower arrangers had been able to lay their hands on. There were only two low steps to be climbed but Colin, solicitous as ever, took his wife's arm to help her up.

The stall holders left their stalls and gathered around to hear the fête declared open. The grass was dry now, the awnings cast dark, hard shadows, not a ripple of breeze disturbed Betty's hat as she stood alongside her husband. The phrase, 'His wife stood by him', came into the mind of all who observed them standing there together.

Traditionally it was a short speech. Everybody wanted to get on with the serious business of buying. 'I shall be even briefer than usual,' Colin promised, 'as my dear wife also has a few words to say.'

They looked up expectantly. How they admired such loyalty. Most people would have drawn the line at speaking on such a day, the fans thought, but not our Betty.

'My friends,' she began, 'this is the seventh year I have attended this fête – for which you all work so hard and give so much – and the last.'

Expressions changed and froze, as children used to be told faces would, if the wind changed direction.

The silence was a palpable thing.

'I shall miss many of you,' the cool, clear voice was saying. 'You have given me your support and sometimes, I think, your affection. And your loyalty. We all have qualities which matter to us more than any others and for me that quality is loyalty. You gave me your loyalty and I thank you for it. My husband has not, and I am leaving him for it. I know that it is a tradition in this party for betrayed wives to stand by their husbands; I do not respect them for it. I think some of them would endure humiliation rather than lose the trappings of being an MP's wife. Others no doubt enjoy the pleasures of martyrdom. For myself I want none of it. I am making this announcement so that what I am doing and why is quite clear. Thank you and goodbye.'

She climbed down the two steps unassisted and walked away. Nobody moved. As if mesmerised, they went on staring at the place where she had been on the dais. But a woman brewing tea in the marquee saw her make for the carpark and drive away.

Kate was waiting for her, the car ready.

'Let's just put your case in the boot,' she said, 'and lock your car up in the garage. Nobody followed you?'

'No. They were too gob-smacked. Colin will have to stay and face the music and the local press won't have a clue where I've gone.'

'All the same, we should be off quickly. Come upstairs and change. I've put some sandwiches on the dressing table and I'll bring you up a coffee.'

Betty was pale, she noticed, and looked weary. She helped her off with the linen dress and hung it up in her wardrobe.

'It rather outclasses my stuff,' she remarked cheerfully, handing over the slacks and shirt, which Betty had brought in the mistaken belief that they looked old and shabby.

'I've fixed up to rent the cottage,' she went on. 'I just said I was coming up with a friend. I've done it before, so nobody will think anything of it.'

'What about your family?' Betty asked on the way downstairs.

'Don't worry, they're all seen to. Daniel and Paulette think I'm going to stay with friends for a week or so. Luke is the only one who knows where we are. Look, I've put a rug and pillow in the back of the car. You just lie on the back seat and get some sleep.'

'Also, I won't be visible to pursuers, no? It's all a bit cloak-and-dagger, isn't it?' Betty said, but all the same she did as she was told and realised, as soon as she lay back, that she was exhausted.

'How long does it take? To get to Netherby, I mean?'

'About four hours if we're lucky and there aren't any hold-ups on the M5. Now just stop worrying about anything and go to sleep. Leave everything to Kate.'

Yes, that's all she wanted to do now, leave everything to Kate. The steady, animal roar of the traffic lulled her, she felt the gentle movement of the car, rocking her to sleep. In a haze she seemed to see scenes from the past twenty-four hours, saw again the dais and all those upturned faces, smiling, uncertain. She heard her own clear voice, like the voice of a stranger, speaking the well-rehearsed words. She felt again the tremble in her legs as she climbed down and set off for the carpark, a short distance that seemed to take for ever.

They swirled about her clouded mind, these vignettes, as she half-dozed. She kept dropping off to sleep, then waking suddenly with a jerk, as if she had tripped and must save herself from falling. Time and again she dozed and jumped back to wakefulness until at last she fell into a deep sleep.

She awoke to the sound of rain. She sat up, puzzled, rubbing her face in her hands.

'How are things back there?' Kate asked.

She yawned, and smiled. 'I feel a lot better for that. Though goodness knows what I'm going to do about it all, Kate.'

'You're not going to make any decisions. You're going to try to forget it for a few days. You're going to think about yourself and we're going to have long walks and—'

'What, in this weather? When did this lot start?'

156

'Just as we were leaving the M5,' Kate said, peering through the sluicing rain. 'It's the sort that goes upwards on the windscreen,' she added. 'But it won't last. It's just a heat storm.'

All the same, she could scarcely see to drive as they made their way between the high walls of the winding road into the village.

'Do we have to go and collect the key?'

'No, Mrs Dingleby's granddaughter said she'd leave it under the scraper by the door.

Although the cottage was called Dale View it was always known as Mrs Dingleby's cottage, long dead though she was.

'I remember going round to Mrs Dingleby's when we were little,' Betty said suddenly. 'Wasn't she the one we used to take dead insects to?'

'That's right. She was a zoologist and knew the names of everything. We used to take flowers and insects round for her to identify. They were usually alive at that stage. Then we'd label them and keep them in jam jars. Till they dried up.'

'She showed us how to blow eggs too.'

'Yes. You had to prick them with a needle at both ends and then you blew.'

'Except that I sucked by mistake and got a mouthful of bad egg and threw up in her kitchen sink.'

'She was a good sort, Mrs Dingleby.'

'I remember.'

And so it came back, the world of their childhood. She hadn't been back here as Kate had, hadn't kept in touch. She had forgotten what it was like when they were part of the countryside, when long summer days were spent on the hills, in the fields, down by the beck, picking unknown wild flowers to take to Mrs Dingleby, chasing dragonflies on the Moss, damming streams, catching minnows and bullheads, levering caddis-flies off stones. Before exams, before ambition, before Colin. Cling to that. Mustn't romanticise, mustn't cheat; it wasn't idyllic at the time. But it was real. Much of what followed wasn't.

'Wait there,' Kate said, drawing up outside the cottage. 'I'll go and unlock. Then you can help me ferry all the stuff indoors. I've brought masses of provisions to save having to shop.'

She didn't demur. Let Kate be in charge, she thought, as she watched her friend make a dash for it up the stone-flagged path of the overgrown garden, retrieve the key from under the scraper, struggle with the ancient lock and, pushing hard against the door, practically fall inside.

The rain was driving horizontally as they unloaded cases and boxes of food. In the distance it seemed to gust like smoke, it was driving so hard. Closer at hand it fell in great beads, crashing against the car.

'I like to see nature asserting herself, don't you?' Kate asked cheerfully.

'Frankly, no,' Betty replied, covering her head with an empty Kleenex box, as she made a dash for the cottage.

Chapter Twenty-six

The next day dawned fine, clear and still. It was the sun, shafting in through the thin, flowered curtains, which woke Betty who lay in bed, wondering for a moment where she was.

I am back in the village of my childhood, she realised, and was suddenly afraid that it might have changed. The wall between her room and Kate's was only a thin partition so, fearful of waking her, she slid from under the patchwork quilt and crept across the wide-planked floor to the window. Leaving the curtains closed, she went and sat behind them on the deep windowseat, curling her long legs under her and wrapping her dressing gown around her shoulders. The trees still dripped in the garden, but there were patches of paler grey on the path where the flagstones were already beginning to dry.

She kept her eyes down on the garden, then let them travel slowly across the road, to the village green and the houses which clustered around it as if they had grown there. No changes here. Well, yes, some. The house where the two old seamstresses, Miss James and Miss Peabody, used to live had had its windows altered and an extension built on. She could still remember the feel of those cold and ancient hands as they fumbled round her neck fitting collars and sleeves. They grumbled a lot about the price of sewing thread and the way they couldn't sleep for the noise on Saturday nights when there was a dance in the village hall.

Outside the old smithy there was now a petrol pump where once a horse used to wait patiently, hoof resting in the blacksmith's hand, while he tapped and chipped. He was a huge, brown man in a long leather apron, who used to ignore her and Kate when they stood watching, savouring the smell of leather and burning hoof. He ignored them too when they crept inside the door to watch as, horses shod, he went back into the smithy and worked the bellows, so that the fire blazed and glowed and sent sparks flying

159

in all directions. He always left a mess of nails and bits of metal outside in the street; the boy who swept the village roads had to sweep it up, grumbling.

In her bedroom too, Kate had got up to look at the morning. Her window had the same view over the village. She too remembered the smithy and the houses around the green. But she had been more recently. She knew that the blacksmith was old and gaunt now, frail and stooping. The boy who swept the streets was a middle-aged man and you could tell by the way he walked that he had back trouble. Miss James and Miss Peabody were sound asleep in the cemetery, undisturbed even on Saturday nights.

Oh yes, she knew there were changes. But the hills could not change. She looked at them last of all and, as always, they surprised her, familiar though they were. Still that amazing lifting of the spirit, still the surprise at the clarity, the perfection of the outline of them, the living green and the gentle, gentle grey. Of course she knew what it would be like, but it always astonished her, the intensity of it. In the same way that, although she knew it would be lovely to see the children again after a parting, there was always a shock of recognition when they rushed towards her, a sudden surge of love, which took her by surprise.

Never before, she thought as she gazed out of the window, had she seen the hills looking quite so fresh and vivid as they did now after last night's cloudburst. The sun caught the upper slopes and sparkled, lighting up some of the stones so that they shone like pools of water. The whole countryside was newly washed and rinsed and, like clean linen, spread out to dry.

Kate, gazing at the hills, realised suddenly that she had brought her friend here not just as a place of refuge, but a place of healing. Surely it was here, if anywhere, that she would find strength to rebuild her life.

There was nobody about as they set off together that first morning. It was Sunday and the village was in church or chapel or bed.

'It doesn't seem so steep now,' Betty remarked as they climbed up the lane. 'Do you remember how Bisto used to dash ahead and stand there waiting impatiently and then come tearing back to us?'

'What happened to him?'

'He died of natural causes when he was twelve. It was the day the family moved to Birmingham.'

She had found him, stretched out, unnaturally still, in his basket in the kitchen. She had knelt on the floor beside him, the tears that poured from her eyes making the wiry black and white hair of his chest all wet. He was her childhood's confidant. She had told him more secrets than anyone else, including Kate.

Everyone had been rushing about that morning, impatient to be off. A dead dog really was the last straw. She could imagine her brothers making a story of it later to their friends, hamming up the trauma of the move, the removal men getting the wardrobe stuck on the landing, and then the punchline, 'And to cap it all, the dog died.'

She had seen her mother having a conspiratorial mutter with the removal men and knew, just from the look of her, that she was asking them to dispose of poor Bisto.

The only person who'd really cared had been Mrs Hough.

'There, there,' she'd said. 'Don't take on. He's gone to a better place. Just put that dust sheet over him and I'll get Mr Hough to give him a decent Christian burial.'

So she had covered him with an old paint-encrusted dust sheet, while Mrs Hough helped herself to another slice of apple pie, left over by the removal men.

'Yes,' Betty told Kate now. 'It was awful when he died, but maybe he'd have hated Birmingham.'

They had reached the brow of the hill. To their left the Boar's Back loomed, long and green with that great tumbling mass of scree at one end.

'Did we really climb that?' Betty asked.

Kate nodded. 'I wouldn't do it now for a king's ransom,' she said.

Betty laughed. 'Nor me. And anyway the price of kings has fallen since we were children.'

They walked without speaking for a while, climbing steadily up the lane that wound its way between dry-stone walls that hid from view the sheep, whose bleating was the only sound that broke the silence of the countryside.

'I'd quite forgotten how peaceful it is here, how still,' Betty said, almost in a whisper. And then added suddenly and more loudly, 'Do you really think we can get away with it?'

'I don't see why not. Nobody down there has any reason to connect you with me. I'll ring Luke this evening and he'll let me know if anyone's been prowling at home. And if they don't trace you to our house, there's no reason why they should come up here.'

'Unless someone in the village—'

'Unlikely. It's not as if anyone will see much of you; you'll be mostly in the cottage or out walking. I truly don't think anyone will take any notice. And if they did realise, I don't believe that there's anyone in Netherby who'd even dream of giving you away. Village people aren't like that.'

Betty smiled. 'Dear old Kate,' she said. 'You always were more trusting than I was.'

'It's more realistic to trust people,' Kate told her, with a touch of irritation in her voice. 'Most people are trustworthy and it's so negative and sterile to go round being suspicious of the world. I hated all that cynicism of the Eighties, all that stuff about everybody having their price and nobody doing anything except for money. Most of the worthwhile things in life aren't done for money. If money was the only motive, who'd write a poem or have a baby? Oh, I'm sorry,' she added suddenly, remembering.

'It's all right. And I take your point. Half the people who believed what you call "all that stuff" have gone bankrupt anyway.'

'All I meant really was that it's more practical to trust the people here and, all right, we might one evening get back to find the cottage surrounded by the press, but let's assume we won't. Let's just enjoy all this while we can. And get you fit for whatever awaits when we do go back.'

'Agreed.'

Now they had reached the point at which the countryside changed, became wilder, the gentler slopes of the hills which surrounded the village giving way to bleaker fells. Sawborough loomed in the distance.

'How about climbing Sawborough one day?' Betty asked. 'Do you think our old bones will make it?'

'I haven't been up there or Cumberside since I was a student, but of course we could do it. Well, after a few days of getting in training.'

So every day they walked on the hills and every evening she rang Luke from the telephone box in the village.

'He seems to think it's all dying down now,' she told Betty towards the end of the week. 'There's a meatier scandal brewing which is diverting the attention of the press. It's really up to you now when you want to go back.'

They had climbed Sawborough and were resting on its lower slopes on their way home. Puffy white clouds moved swiftly across a clear blue sky, casting shadows on the green hillside, as she lay alongside Betty on the short turf, gazing up into space. They had often lain like this when they were children, she remembered, but she didn't remember ever feeling as stiff as this, she thought wryly as she shifted her limbs, trying to adjust them to the contours of the hard earth beneath the springy, sheep-cropped grass.

'I think I can face it now,' Betty said suddenly. 'Going back I mean, dealing with the press if I must, sorting out the divorce.'

Kate hesitated.

'Betty,' she said slowly. 'Are you sure you want that? I mean that you don't want to have another try with Colin?'

'Quite sure. You see—' she sat up, as if to think better. 'It's not just the Claire business, silly girl that she was. It's more than that. Coming back here has helped to clarify it all in my mind. There's time to think here, to think deeply. How else can you think but deeply, among these hills? I never was really right for Colin, you know. We weren't the same sort of person. I thought we were, at least I thought we ought to be. I'd worked it all out, you see. I didn't just marry on an impulse.'

Like I did, Kate thought. And yet it worked for me. There's no justice.

'And when his way of doing things seemed to be so successful, I think I was overawed by it all. I just accepted things which I didn't really feel in my bones to be right. But there were such pressures, and he was surrounded by people – we both were – who thought the same. They all egged each other on, all those yuppies. Things were said and done that people would have been ashamed to say and do a decade earlier. I was uneasy among it, but I managed to suppress what I really felt. I'm not very proud of myself in those years really.'

Kate was sitting up too now.

'Others have more to be ashamed of than you have,' she pointed out.

'No, I should have known better. You weren't impressed by it all, Kate, were you?'

'No,' she hesitated. 'But then I was in a different world. A more real world and I knew the damage that was being done because Luke and Jack and lots of our friends were always worried about it.'

'And Nell too, she always said it was false, all the boom and bust business of the Eighties. Another South Sea Bubble, she called it. If only they'd listened to people like her, they might not have made such a mess of things.'

They sat in silence for a while. It was hotter now up here and very still except for the occasional bleating of sheep and the sound of crickets chirruping invisibly in the short grass.

'And babies?' Kate asked gently.

'It's very strange,' Betty said. 'And I don't know if you'll understand this, I hardly do myself. When I was in love with Colin I desperately wanted his child. And I was in love with him, the approving or disapproving thing didn't alter that. Now that I'm not in love with him any more, I find I just don't mind in the same way. I've thought a lot about it, Kate, and I think I can just accept it now. It's sad, but bearable. The panic, the desperate need seems to have gone.'

'So what next?'

'I've thought a lot about that too. I'm coming up to forty, time to plan ahead. Of course I could go back to my old career in the City; it was a great experience and fascinating work. We dealt, you know, with complex legal problems about taxation and trusts and huge estates, all very rich clients whether corporate or individual. Vast sums of money were involved. But once you get away from it, take a detached look, it all seems rather pointless. What difference did a million either way make to them anyway?'

'So?'

Betty looked at her and smiled.

'So?' she mimicked. 'So, my friend, I just feel I'd like to put my skills to better use. I'd like to find myself a partnership in a smaller practice where I could help real people with real problems. Well, perhaps real is the wrong word, the other problems were real enough, but you know to help with things that really matter, that make a difference to people's lives. So many people now urgently need legal advice, small firms bankrupted, people in danger of losing their homes, all sorts of people paying the price of the Eighties. In a sense I contributed to the damage that was done then, and I'd like to contribute something to putting it right or at least repairing some of the damage.'

Kate was listening hard, nodding approval now and then, and when Betty had finished, she said, 'That's marvellous and I know you'll do it.'

She had watched this week as every day her friend was more relaxed, the lines of stress smoothed away, and now her face was glowing with the sun and wind and mountain air. She had always been poised with a brittle kind of elegance but now there was a sureness and confidence about the way she spoke that made Kate say again, 'I just know that you'll do it.'

The shadows cast by the dry-stone walls were lengthening, the sun was beginning its slow descent to the west, over Cumberside.

'We ought to be getting back,' she said. 'But, Betty, while we're talking about this, I must—' she paused.

'Go on.'

'I don't know how to put it. Apologise isn't quite the right word. But I've always felt badly about Claire. I mean I was the one who told you she was looking for a job. Chrissie had told me she was and—'

'Forget it,' Betty interrupted. 'If it hadn't been Claire, it would have been somebody else. I can see now, with hindsight, that he was just the sort who needed an affair to boost his ego. You'd never think so, but it was rather a frail little ego.'

Kate nodded but said nothing, remembering how she had always thought him a hollow man. As they got up and gathered their things together, she said, 'The other one I'm really sorry for in all this is Chrissie. She'll take it to heart so.'

'But it wasn't her fault,' Betty said, surprised. Then added, 'Still, you know her better than I do.'

'She'll think it was her fault. Parents – well, Chrissie's sort of parent – always feel responsible for what their children do.'

'Even when they're Claire's age?'

'At any age. Once a parent, always a parent. That's what's so awesome about it.'

'In that case, maybe I'm well out of it,' Betty said, as they set off back down the lane.

Chapter Twenty-seven

Lethargically, Chrissie brushed her greying hair, wordlessly, she climbed into bed. Jack watched her, his heart aching.

'Come here,' he said, taking her in his arms.

'Oh, Jack,' she said, 'I just can't get over it. Our Claire to do such a thing.'

Every day at work she had tried to keep it out of her mind, concentrate on what she was doing to the exclusion of all else. She had always managed it before, but this business of Claire was of a different order of things. Flesh of her flesh, she shared her guilt; it could not be cast off.

'And I just can't bear to think of poor Betty,' she said now and burst into tears.

He let her cry, stroked her hair and shoulders, held her tight, saying nothing. He understood all she felt, and knew that there were no consoling words. So they lay close together, sharing their grief.

But when she said, 'I keep wondering where I went wrong, Jack. What should we have done that was different?' he drew away slightly and said firmly, 'No, Chrissie. We didn't fail her. She was brought up to know the difference between right and wrong, as we were, as Sarah was. It's no good blaming yourself. Adding guilt won't help anyone.'

'But I can't help it, Jack. I just keep asking myself *why*.'

He longed to help her. He knew that Claire had often hurt her in the past and she had accepted that calmly, knowing that the joys that children bring must be paid for in pain, but this was different, this had hurt other people. That was what Chrissie couldn't bear.

After a while he said thoughtfully, 'I know one should never blame circumstances and that we're all responsible for what we do, but remember she went into a world that was quite unlike ours when she was very impressionable. She was immature, you know, compared with Sarah at the same age. She needed more time to grow up. But instead she went suddenly, quite unprepared, into that false world, full of lies and deceit, and she was impressed by it.'

'But why, why be impressed by it? Why couldn't she just – reject it?'

'I suppose she was overawed by them all. These were powerful men, you know. Look, Chrissie, I heard a cabinet minister, who'd had an affair, saying in an interview on the radio the other day, "Everybody does it, don't they? Why should politicians be the only ones who're expected to be squeaky clean?" You and I know he's lying. Everyone does *not* behave like that and he's only saying it because he feels less guilty if he smears everybody else. He's like some yobbo saying, "Of course I nick things, my mates nick things, everybody nicks things, don't they?" But perhaps Claire didn't know it, perhaps she really thought that theirs was the real world and that we were the ones who were out of touch with real life.'

She tried to follow what he was saying, but this kind of reasoning never made much sense to Chrissie. She saw things more simply.

'But that's no excuse, Jack,' she insisted. 'And she is our daughter and we *are* responsible. Even poor Kate feels badly because she was the one who suggested Claire should work for Colin in the first place. So how much worse should we feel?'

'I'm not excusing what she did, my darling. I'm only trying to make you see there were reasons. I've had more to do with men like that than you have and I know how overbearing they can be with their power and money. Politicians nowadays don't feel guilty about anything. It's part of their way of life not to take responsibility for the consequences of what they do. They won't apologise for having an affair any more than they'd apologise for the Poll Tax. And if you know you're not going to feel guilty, you don't have a conscience about doing anything.'

'But Claire wasn't like that. She always *did* have a conscience. Things worried her. We often talked about them. I remember thinking how much she'd changed when she said she could make more money in half an hour buying and selling shares than she could in ten days delivering the mail. It wasn't a good way for her to be thinking, was it? I should have realised then. Maybe if I'd taken more notice of that—'

'Stop it, Chrissie, stop blaming yourself,' he cut in firmly, almost angrily. Then he went on more gently, 'You'd be better to have it out with her now, really talk to her about it all. You haven't yet, have you?'

'No, I can't seem to bring myself to, somehow. Well, I did try at the beginning.'

Oh yes, she'd tried, that first night, tried to reach out to her daughter, but Claire didn't even seem sorry: tight-lipped and obstinate, she just wanted it all sorted out as if none of it was of her doing.

'And then, you know,' Chrissie went on, 'we were all so busy trying to avoid the press and publicity and getting her away from here, that there was no time to think about what really mattered. And now that she's back she just seems to want to stay in her room and I've been at work anyway . . .'

Her voice trailed off. Even to Jack she couldn't explain the pain of it. She seemed to be seeing her daughter through a stranger's eyes and not liking what she saw. It was a kind of hell, this non-loving. Claire had always been difficult, critical and changeable, but it had all been on the surface, nothing had disturbed the love that lay between them, deep and assured, the one certain thing. But now there was just a terrible, desolate wasteland of estrangement. She knew she had lost the will even to try to reach across it to her daughter.

'Please talk to her, Chrissie. She's suffered too, you know. And the times were against her. She was a victim of the Eighties, in her own way, just as much as, say, our poor Mrs Rawley. So do try. We both love her, but you're the one who can get through to her if anyone can. And she's so unhappy.'

She hadn't thought of it like that. She had thought of her daughter as the cause of all this misery, not the sharer in it. Strange that for once she hadn't thought of the pain her own child was suffering.

'I'll try, Jack,' she said. 'I'll try again.'

She lay in his arms, trying to think what she would say to her. She thought of her own parents and what they would have felt if – but, no, it was unthinkable. Try to concentrate on her own daughter, hate the sin but not the sinner, not of course that the word hate came into it, but blame, yes. Confused and tearful, she eventually fell into an uneasy sleep.

*   *   *

Claire was lying in bed when her mother went into her room the next morning.

'I've brought you a cup of tea,' she said, putting it down on the chest of drawers by the bedside.

Claire lifted herself on one elbow. She looked dreadful, Chrissie noticed, very dark under the eyes, her face white and drawn. Quite plain she looked.

'Thanks, Mum,' she said humbly.

She looked at her mother and saw that her face and hair were grey and there were deep, dark shadows, like bruises, around her eyes. She looked old and very tired. I've done this to her, Claire thought, and burst into tears.

Chrissie sat on the bed and took her daughter in her arms, overwhelmed with compassion for her. There was no need to think what to say; the barrier was broken down, the deep, old love flowed between them and they clung to each other. How simple it was.

'Oh, Mum, I'm so sorry.'

This from Claire who had never found it easy, even when she was little, to say she was sorry. Chrissie rocked her in her arms and it was as if a great weight had been lifted, such was her relief that they were close together again.

'I really loved him, Mum. I think I still do. And I knew it was wrong and I was deceiving everyone but somehow it seemed right at the time, inevitable.'

'People always fool themselves like that, love,' Chrissie told her. 'Perhaps I should have talked to you more about these things.'

'As if I'd have listened!'

'That's true.'

'You'll never forgive me, will you?'

'It's not for me to forgive. It's Betty that you've hurt.'

'I know and she was always kind to me.' She began to cry again. 'And she'd given up her career for— him. And she'd worked hard for— him. And she was a friend of your friend.'

Chrissie let her cry for a while and then asked, 'So what are you going to do about it?'

'Do you think that if I wrote and said I was sorry and asked her to try to forgive me – eventually, I mean – she'd just be angry? Tear the letter up and send me back the pieces?'

'No. I don't think she'd do that.'

She picked up the cup and handed it to her daughter.

'Drink your tea before it gets cold,' she said.

She sat watching while Claire obediently drank the tepid tea.

Then she said, 'We think, your dad and me, that you've got to look ahead now. You can't undo what's been done, but you can make a better job of your life in the future.'

'I haven't been able to think about it. My mind's been full of— Colin.'

'Then empty your mind of Colin,' her mother told her. 'He's no place there.'

'Yes, I'll try.'

'You mustn't hang about the house any more. You need work, even if it's just something temporary.'

'Do you think I might apply to be a helper at Sarah's school?'

'It's worth asking. Now get up and have a shower. Then have a talk with Sarah.'

'I did try, Mum,' Sarah said a few days later. 'I know they're looking for somebody, but the Head said that she thought perhaps in view of what's happened, Claire wasn't quite suitable. I'm sorry, Mum, I know it hurts. The Head's a lovely, tolerant person, but there has been such a lot of gossip and she has to think of the mums.'

'Have you told Claire?'

'Not yet. I can't face it. I mean, poor kid, it's pretty humiliating.'

'She's got to face it, Sarah. She's got to accept the consequences of what she did, humiliation included. She'll be the stronger for it in the end.'

Sarah was surprised at her mother's reaction; from the gentle Chrissie, this was pretty harsh stuff. But, 'You're right, Mum,' she said. 'And really I think she might be better to get back to studying. Law maybe. She's a good brain and the discipline would be good.'

'You mean a solicitor? Like Betty?'

'Well, a solicitor, but not like Betty,' Sarah said, smiling. Then she added thoughtfully, 'Claire's changed in the last few days. I really think she's going to be different now. I don't know how it's come about but she seems more mature somehow. You know how she suddenly went very grown-up when she was working for Colin? Well, it was false, wasn't it? She wasn't really mature at all, just sophisticated.'

'Yes, I know exactly what you mean.'

'But now she really does seem more truly adult. I think she's beginning to sort herself out at last.'

'Oh, yes, she'll be all right now,' her mother said, and added simply, 'She's repented.'

Chapter Twenty-eight

The Constituency Association in Boxley was once again divided. The new Prime Minister had won a General Election and could now claim to hold office in his own right. That was cause for jubilation in party headquarters throughout the land, except of course in those constituencies where sitting members had lost their seats, of which Colin's was one.

There were those who said bitterly that, if he'd had whole-hearted support, he could have won. After all, they argued, the two women involved in the scandal had behaved sensibly, they hadn't sold their stories to the press or anything like that. The divorce had been a discreet affair, there were no children involved, which was important because though voters might be persuaded that unfaithfulness in their politician was a mere peccadillo and what you might expect if you knew how the cookie crumbled, they did tend to get upset about causing shame and misery to innocent children. Women particularly got upset about it. But there was nothing like that in poor old Colin's case and dammit the man had done well, got on in parliament and it's a bonus to have a Minister, albeit a junior one, for your MP; there'd been no chance of that with his predecessor.

Others took a different line, particularly the Betty fans. There was no addressing and stuffing of envelopes by them this time round, no delivering of pamphlets, no sitting as tellers outside polling booths on the day. Grim-faced, they conceded their vote to him but nothing – absolutely nothing – more. They felt a certain triumph when he lost. It showed what a difference their support made. Perhaps the hierarchy would pay a bit more attention to their views next time.

For Colin, defeat had its compensations. Bankruptcy was certainly the best way out of his financial difficulties; it was a formality nowadays, nothing shaming about it, just a means of damage limitation. But of course it wouldn't have been possible if he had still been an MP. Now that the uncertainty was over, he could get on with sorting it all out. Fortunately he had friends in the City.

Now also he could get on with his plans for disposing of the Manor House. So, on a pleasantly fresh and sunny June morning, he met the developer, a Mr Weevil, outside the main entrance to the house.

Mr Weevil was a round-faced, doughy-looking man. His eyes were small and very dark and had the look of currants pressed rather too deeply into a teacake. There was a knowing, calculating look in those sharp little eyes as they darted about the buildings, assessing how these old bricks and mortar could be converted into cash. For this was his speciality: he spent his time now devising ways of converting stables, making mansions into houses, houses into flats, flats into bedsitters. The more units you could convert into, he reckoned, the more money there was in it.

Plump and of medium height, obsequiousness made him seem shorter than he actually was, for he was constantly ducking and bending. He liked his clients to feel that they were making the decisions, that all the ideas were theirs. It wasn't difficult; some of them might speak in a grand way of not wanting to spoil the character of the place, but when it came to the crunch they were as greedy as the next man. He had no reason to think that the ex-MP would be any different.

'Where would you like to start?' he asked Colin now. Put the ball in his court.

'I thought the outbuildings?' Colin suggested, leading the way across the old poultry yard to the courtyard beyond where three stables, built of brick under slate roofs, faced them.

'I thought we should get three nice flats there,' he said.

'Three?' Mr Weevil pursed his lips. 'Have you anything against six, then?'

'No,' Colin said, surprised. 'I mean, I just thought three would be the maximum you could fit in.'

'Not if you had three downstairs and then put three up in the roof.'

'You mean each one entirely in the roof space?'

'Agreed. Fortunately it's not a listed building so we can do what we like with the roof. A bit hot in the summer and cold in winter

maybe but it's amazing what modern insulation can do. You'd need
an extra staircase, of course, but the additional cost is minimal. I
reckon you'd get two-thirds again, in return on your investment.'

'That can't be bad,' Colin said.

'Drive – in there, I imagine is what you have in mind, isn't it?'
Mr Weevil said, turning his decision into a question.

'Oh, well, yes. But the trees?'

'No problem, modern equipment pulls 'em up in no time. Easy
as drawing a tooth. Parking won't be a problem either. Cobbles a
bit rough but we'll leave them until the building's finished and then
cover them with asphalt. Unless you have other ideas of finish, of
course?'

'No, just plain asphalt, I think.'

'Then we'll stroll down to the paddock, shall we? Have a look
at the Lodge first?'

'Yes. It's let, as I told you. To the village schoolmistress.'

'I checked the lease. No problem about getting her out. Three
units there, I reckon. You see, it can be sold along with the paddock
scheme. I think no more than eight houses in the paddock.'

'What about planning? Do you have any thoughts about that?
Will it be easy to get permission?'

'No problem. But they must be up-market, executive properties.
Georgian to fit the style of the Manor. You know the kind of thing,
imitation glazing bars in the windows, moulded plastic panels in
the doors, all very tasteful. Pillars, of course. Polystyrene pillars
are very gracious and not expensive.'

He gazed across the paddock to the road, to the avenue of poplar
trees. 'The entrance would be down there, then up through those
trees, entering the estate between two pillars, artistically designed,
of course. Then each house would have its own drive, curving, if
possible, in a nice executive sweep.'

The greedy little eyes glistened as he pictured it.

'Yes, very nice, I think it will look, very tasteful,' he said.

'Not less than two hundred and fifty thousand apiece. If times
improve could be higher. Money's not short round here. There's
always demand for houses of this quality.'

They turned and began to walk back to the Manor.

'Now what had you in mind for the house itself?' he asked
Colin.

'Nothing really, I'd just assumed it would stay as it is.'

'Probably right. That's the principle behind the asset stripping, keep what's useful to you, sell off the rest. But while we're here we might just consider how it could be divided, if it came to it.'

So they went from room to room, imagining partitions and staircases, pulling down this wall, lowering that ceiling, while Mr Weevil did sums with a swiftly jabbing plump finger on his calculator.

In the master bedroom they stood looking down the long vista of poplars to the wooded valley beyond.

'That's where the road to the paddock would come in,' Mr Weevil said. 'You get the best view of it from here.'

'And the trees? The poplar walk?'

'There isn't a preservation order on them. I checked that. Still, just as well to get them down quickly before some do-gooder runs round to the council to get one slapped on them.'

He looked thoughtfully down at the valley.

'Of course there's money in trees, you know. We might find a buyer. It's amazing what people will pay for a mature tree. I'll get a price for them,' he said, nodding towards the poplar grove and making a note in his Filofax.

'Well, I think we've covered a lot of ground today, Mr Baker,' he said. 'Very satisfactory. I hope you think so too, sir?'

'Indeed, yes. I'm very grateful to you for all your advice. Have you time for a drink before you go?'

'Wouldn't say no,' Mr Weevil told him.

'Then we'll go down to my study.'

'Nice place you've got here,' Mr Weevil said, following him down the broad staircase, momentarily forgetting the situation. 'I mean I hadn't realised until I came,' he went on hastily, recollecting himself, 'that you still have all your furniture in it.'

'Oh, yes, I still use the place,' Colin told him. 'But of course I shall empty it now.'

He'd have to contact Betty, he thought as he poured the drinks, and ask her to come and take what was hers. She'd said she wouldn't take anything while he was still living there. She'd been very reasonable about it, about everything really. She'd made no conditions, wanted no money. He found that rather chilling; a bit of bitterness would have seemed more natural somehow.

Mr Weevil's plump little hand was raising the glass to him, Mr Weevil's little blackcurrant eyes were watching him.

'Cheers,' Mr Weevil said.

For a moment Colin's mind went curiously blank and he wondered what this vulgar little man was doing in his study. Then he recovered himself and raised his glass.

'Cheers, Mr Weevil,' he replied.

Chapter Twenty-nine

'The Manor House is up for sale,' Betty told Kate on the telephone. 'And I have to go back and sort things out. You see, I left him all the furniture while he lived there, but now, of course, I've got to arrange for some of my things to be sent to Exeter when the house is cleared. I don't care about a lot of the stuff but there are things like my desk and—'

'Of course I'll come with you,' Kate interrupted, not deceived by the lightness of tone.

'Oh, would you? Could you spare the time? I'm afraid it's a bit urgent.'

'Like when?'

'Like tomorrow.'

'That's all right. I'll meet you there, shall I? Oh—'

'What?'

'I've just remembered that Chrissie and Nell are coming over for the day. Don't worry, I'll cancel them. They'll understand.'

'No, don't do that. Bring them along. We can take a picnic. They needn't come inside if they don't want to, but the grounds will be lovely and the forecast's good.'

Kate hesitated, not sure if this calmness, this collectedness, was genuine. Betty always managed to seem in control of her feelings, but surely even she was going to find it hard to bear this breaking up of her old home. And in the presence of Claire's mother too.

'If you're quite sure? I mean do you really want other people around?'

'I'm sure I'm sure. Did you know that I'm taking Claire on as a trainee?'

'What, with you, in Exeter?'

'That's right. She's done well in her post-graduate law course and now has two years to do as a trainee before she's qualified.'

'Oh, Betty—'

179

She had no words. It was just incredible.

'"Oh, Betty", what?'

'I think you're amazing, that's what. And rather wonderful really.'

'It's only common sense. She's an intelligent girl, just the sort I was looking for. And she needs what I can offer her, so it suits us both. If we didn't do what suits us both just because of Colin, we'd really be making him seem more important than he actually is.'

'All the same, I couldn't have done it, not in your shoes, I couldn't. But it's a marvellous rounding off,' she added thoughtfully.

Increasingly, Betty had observed, Kate saw things in a novelist's way, rounding off events, creating symmetry, as if the messiness of life was somehow more acceptable if you could knock it into some kind of artistic shape.

She laughed now. 'I almost knew you'd say that. How's the book world?'

'Well, do you know, I think it might be changing. All that commercial talk of the Eighties, nothing mattering except profits and never say the word "book", just the "product", à l'américain, is beginning to go out of fashion. So it could be that the likes of me will become publishable again.'

'But will you have anything to publish? I mean, you gave up writing, didn't you?'

Kate laughed.

'No,' she said, 'I didn't. I gave up trying to get anything published. But I went on writing just the same. I wrote, you know, as I've always done, what I had to write, not what someone said I ought. Then, when I'd got the manuscript as right as I could make it, I wrapped it up and put it in a drawer. Three of them in the end.'

'But Kate, how could you go on like that, without any response? I couldn't have done. I mean, wasn't it terribly discouraging?'

'Yes, it was, but I just plodded on regardless. Mind you, I felt a bit guilty about not getting a job to help keep the family. Money was short, but Luke wouldn't hear of my giving up. He's always backed me.'

'And you say *I'm* amazing!'

'It's had a happy ending. The first of the three is coming out next year. I'm checking the copy-editing now.'

'Oh, Kate, I'm so glad. Congratulations! Tell me all about it tomorrow. And, Kate, publishable or not, thank you.'

'I disagreed with practically everything she did,' Nell said, as they sat by the lake eating a late picnic lunch. 'But I could never have treated her like that.'

It was nearly two years since the Prime Minister had fallen but people still talked as if her dismissal was recent.

'I mean, to be stabbed in the back not by her enemies but by her friends! And they were the ones who had egged her on.'

'Fitting, though, don't you think?' asked Kate, still with her novelist's need to see the symmetry of things.

'But to be the only Prime Minister who's ever been thrown out while in office – the shame of it!'

'Those who live by skulduggery shall perish by skulduggery,' Kate misquoted. 'There is a very pleasing kind of poetic justice in it.'

'Artistic detachment makes you surprisingly callous at times,' Betty told her.

Kate laughed and said, 'I suppose we ought to go and finish off the good work indoors now?'

'Afraid so,' Betty agreed, swallowing the last of her coffee and handing the cup to Chrissie.

Somehow, even on a picnic, Chrissie always seemed to be in charge of the housekeeping.

'Can Nell and I help?' she offered as she packed cups and plates into baskets. 'With lists or anything?'

'No, thanks, Chrissie. There's only upstairs to do now and there's much less furniture up there. We bought mainly new stuff for all those bedrooms, so it will just go to the saleroom.'

'Us oldies will sit and be lazy in the sunshine,' Nell said, taking Chrissie's arm and leading her towards a bench under the weeping willow.

So they sat there quietly reminiscing while the younger pair toured the house, listing items of furniture, tying labels on to chair legs, sticking tickets under tables and desks.

It must be awful for her, Kate thought, not for the first time that day, all this dividing up of everything that once was shared. There must be happy memories stored here, ghosts of other times. But Betty went about it methodically, facing each room

181

in turn, rooms where she and Colin had once eaten, chatted, slept.

They did the master bedroom last.

'I think there's only a little bedside table in here,' Betty said, as she opened the shutters. 'And the small bookcase.'

'Oh, I remember that. It was by your bed in Netherby,' Kate said, running her hand along the top shelf of the little walnut bookcase and precipitating a cloud of dust. 'It was the one I chose books from at Christmas,' she added, rubbing her hand on her trousers.

'That's right. And it still has some of the treasures I hid from you,' Betty admitted. 'And I still wouldn't part with any of them.'

She tied on the pink label which marked the bookcase for Exeter.

'I just hope the removal men understand the system,' she said.

'Will you come to see the things packed up?'

'No, I'll be at the receiving end.'

She crossed over to the window.

'I'd almost forgotten what a view this is,' she said.

Kate joined her and they stood looking out over the park. The lawns looked less neglected from this distance. Maybe most things look better from a distance, Betty thought, as she allowed herself to gaze out for the last time over the countryside, to glimpse the lake and see beyond it the valley and the distant hills. She remembered standing there with Colin, remembered quiet evening walks together round the lake. She dismissed such memories. Look to the future, Betty.

'Betty,' Kate began.

'Yes?'

'I heard a rumour – truly I wasn't listening to gossip – but you know what the grapevine is like.'

'Go on.'

'People were saying that the developers were moving in. I suppose they only have to recognise a car or van and they think Something's Going On at The Manor.'

'Nothing's Going On at The Manor,' Betty told her. 'But it might have done. For once Madam Rumour got it right. But Colin forgot one small but important fact.'

'Which was?'

'When we bought it, he put it, for complicated financial reasons, in my name.'

'He *forgot*? Forgot a thing like that?'

'I know. But remember he had other things on his mind. There was the scandal and the press, there were all sorts of crises in the constituency. Then there was the election. Also he's shrewd about details but has a way of missing the point sometimes. Anyway, legally he can't do what he likes with the Manor.'

'I'm so glad. Because it's a lovely old house, and the grounds belong with the buildings. They should be kept all of a piece.'

'He'll have half the money, of course, but I'll be in charge of how and to whom it's sold. There'll be no chipping off of bits and pieces just to make a quick profit. So no, Colin won't be able to do what he likes with the Manor.'

She turned again to look out over the trees and the valley beyond.

'An old house is like a country, Kate,' she said slowly. 'It doesn't belong absolutely to any temporary owner. They have charge of it, but it outlives them. They're really only caretakers. A government doesn't own a country either. It hasn't the right to make pickings. There's no undoing what was done to this country and Colin had a hand in that, but at least I can stop it happening on a small scale here.'

She stood for a moment looking out, then she closed the shutters, gently folding the wooden panels together, lifting the metal bar across them, dropping the little iron peg that kept it in place. Then together she and Kate crossed the darkened room and went downstairs to join their friends in the evening sunshine.

They met them coming back towards the house.

'It was getting just a bit too cool for sitting,' Nell told her, 'so we thought we'd have a stroll until you were ready.'

'Shall we all have a walk around the grounds before we go home?' Betty suggested. 'You haven't been in the walled garden, have you? Where all the fruit and vegetables are?'

'I didn't even know there was one,' Kate said indignantly. 'You never told me.'

'I was never very interested really. And the gardener did it all. Anyway, you'll see it now,' she added, leading the way round to the back of the house.

If I'd known about the kitchen garden, Kate thought as she

followed her, I wouldn't have taken all those vegetables to London, and if I hadn't taken the vegetables we wouldn't have gone to the flat, and if we hadn't gone to the flat, Betty wouldn't have found out about Claire. Then the whole plot would have been different and this story might have had a happier ending.

Or would it? No, it would all have come out eventually, more slowly, less dramatically maybe, but it would have ended the same because Colin was destined to be an Eighties whizz kid and a Nineties failure, and Betty would have got back to being an independent woman because that was her nature and Claire, with parents like Jack and Chrissie, would have sorted herself out in the end somehow or other.

'I thought you wanted to see this place?' she heard Betty calling and realised that she had lagged behind the others.

She caught up with them just as Betty managed to push back a rusty iron bolt and force open the heavy door in the ivy-clad archway which led into the walled garden.

All the plants had long since gone to seed. Ancient brassicas and purple flowering broccoli branched out in green candelabras bedecked with yellow candles. The withered remains of ancient runner beans drooped from their poles, while greener convolvulus climbed healthily up their stems. Nettles and rose bay willow herb flourished among them, tangled with yarrow and tansy. Creeping buttercup, silverweed and plantain carpeted the ground and poppies splashed the plot with brilliant red and yellow petals.

'Nettles only grow where there's plenty of nitrogen, so it shows it's good soil,' Kate remarked irrelevantly, perhaps seeking to console.

The fruit cage had collapsed and what remained was only held up at one side by raspberry canes. Straggling branches of gooseberry and currant bushes pushed their way through the netting so that thorns and net and branch were inextricably interwoven. Birds flew in and out, swooping down on the once forbidden fruit, which was wild now and theirs for the taking.

The women walked quietly round the perimeter of the garden, past the espaliers of apples and pears which grew against the south wall and the fan-trained plums and peaches on the west. Old and trained for many a year, these trees could survive a few years of neglect.

The air was fresher now and, as they walked, they could feel the heat coming off the walls, for the soft old bricks had absorbed the warmth of the sun all day and were giving it back now in the cool of the evening. Kate let her hand linger on the brickwork, appreciating how the warmth of it must ripen the fruit that lay close to the wall.

They left by a path that led under a rose pergola, unpruned but heavy with roses, that sweetly scented the evening air.

'Let's do a detour down the poplar avenue,' Betty said. 'It's lovely in the evening when you can smell the leaves.'

The sun was lower in the sky and casting longer shadows across the grass as they turned into the avenue of poplars, great old trees, shorter now than their own shadows. Starlings were gathering in the branches, their ceaseless chatter, as they crowded together, somehow not disturbing but rather intensifying the peace of the evening.

Snatches of their conversation mingled with the birdsong as the four women walked back towards the house.

'I can't see why they bothered changing leaders,' Kate said, yawning. 'This lot seem to be carrying on in much the same way.'

'You can't really blame the Prime Minister,' Nell said charitably. 'He's only the poor chap in charge of the henhouse when all his predecessor's chickens have come home to roost.'

'That reminds me,' Kate said, 'I'm keeping hens now. Old-fashioned ones like we used to have, Leghorns and Rhode Island Reds. What's so funny?'

Nell went on laughing, but Chrissie said, 'Yes, we used to have them on the farm, Rhode Islands. I liked their brown eggs best of all.'

Betty said nothing; she saw again a little black and white terrier standing triumphantly in the middle of a hen run, watched by two frightened children. She glanced at Kate. She too was remembering, trying to recognise herself and Betty in those children. She failed. She put the idea away to think about later.

Thus they walked between the trees, talking in the relaxed, desultory way of old friends, while the evening sun slanted across their path so that they walked now in sunshine, now in shadow.

Thomas (10)
Wullock
Hall (19)
Wilkinson
6·7·9 r
OLWM R

LL 60